The Girl Below Stairs

a Victorian romance saga

HOPE DAWSON

www.hopedawson.com

To girls and women everywhere
– past and present –
living in toil and hardship
yet never giving up hope
and always striving for a better tomorrow.

Chapter One

Bethnal Green, 1875

A heavy downpour battered the streets of London, while angry flashes of lightning lit up the lead-coloured clouds in the sky. The rain washing over the cobblestones caused the going to be slippery and treacherous – a condition made even more dangerous by the lashing wind.

Through this dark and vicious storm, straining against the violence of the elements, two miserable figures slowly battled their way towards a cluster of buildings that loomed further down in the street. They were mother and daughter, and if anyone could have been bothered to pay them a closer look, the onlooker would have commiserated at the sad spectacle.

The mother couldn't have been much older than thirty, although she might as well have been an old crone, from the rundown looks of her. She could hardly stand on her feet, so her little girl had to support her.

"We're nearly there, Mother," the girl said. "Just a few more yards and then we'll be safe and dry."

The only reply the woman was able to produce came in the form of a nasty cough that sounded like her lungs were about to burst from her chest.

"Not very far now, Mother. Please be strong. The nurses at the workhouse will be able to help you."

Drenched to the bone and shivering with cold, they finally arrived at the large door of the main building. With some effort, the girl banged the heavy iron knocker against the door a few times. While they waited, her mother suffered another violent coughing fit.

The girl was just about to knock once more, when a grumpy man came to the door, holding it open only as far as was needed for him to stick his head out.

"Who comes knocking in this foul weather?" he demanded, displeased at being called away from his little stove in the hallway.

"I am Stella Reed, sir," the girl said. "And this is my mother. We are destitute and we have nowhere else to go."

The porter sighed and opened the door a bit wider. "I suppose you'd better come in then. But make it quick. You're letting all the heat out."

"Thank you, sir."

Stella tried to help her mother over the doorstep and into the warm hallway. Muttering, the doorman took the woman's other arm and pulled her inside.

"Thank you for your help, sir," Stella smiled. "Most kind of you."

"Only trying to keep the rain and the cold out, girl. What's wrong with your grandmother then?"

"She's not my grandmother, sir. She's my mother. But she's very poorly."

As if to prove her daughter's point, Stella's mother suddenly coughed and wheezed loudly, making the porter jump back.

"Heavens above! That's the sound of death, that is." He kept his distance and tried to cover his mouth and nose with part of his overcoat.

The girl visibly winced at the mention of the word death. "Oh, please don't say that, sir. We've already lost my father and both my siblings."

"Were they sick like that as well?"

"Yes, sir. My little brother was the first to get it, and then my baby sister." She hung her head. "They didn't last very long."

The porter wasn't taking his eyes off her mother, suspicious of the woman's next coughing fit. "You sound fine though," he told Stella.

"Yes, sir. I've had it too, shortly after Father got it. But I wasn't too ill, and I got better. Papa though... He wasn't as lucky."

"And now your mother has it?"

Another hacking cough answered that question.

"Can my mother sit down by the fire for a while, sir?"

"Help yourselves," the porter nodded, continuing to keep his distance. "But the workhouse isn't in the habit of taking in every random stray that wanders in from the street, you know. Haven't you got a home to go to, or any relatives to look after you?"

"There's only Mother and I, sir. And shortly after Father died, they took away everything we owned. They even took away all my books!"

"You poor girl. Took away your books, eh? Fancy that. What is this world coming to?"

Stella was too young to understand what sarcasm was, or even what it sounded like. But she knew she didn't like this man's tone of voice. She didn't care much for his cruel, unsmiling eyes either.

"Are you sure you haven't got any means to support yourselves? Because, quite frankly, you don't sound like the average street urchin to me, little girl."

Stella felt insulted. "Mother always insisted I learned to read and write," she said. "But when Father fell ill, he couldn't go into work. And then Mother got it too. By the time we had buried my siblings and my father, we didn't have any more money. That's when the men came and took everything we had."

She was still angry at the injustice when she told the story.

"And then our landlord threw us out on the street, because we couldn't pay the rent. I told him my mother was sick, but he didn't care. He told us to sleep outside or to come here."

The porter sighed. He had heard these stories so many times before, the sheer tragedy of them didn't really affect him anymore. For him, it was just a job. A boring, poorly paid, and tedious job.

"I'll fetch the Matron," he grumbled. "She'll take care of you. Just wait here."

He disappeared, and eventually came back with a woman who scared Stella because she looked so big and severe. Would everyone at the workhouse be this cold and grim, she wondered?

But the Matron was accompanied by a nurse, and that gave Stella hope they had done the right thing by coming to this infamous place of last resort.

"What have we here?" the Matron asked, studying Stella and her mother as if they were a pair of flea-ridden dogs that had come strolling in, attracted by the promise of free sausages.

When Stella's mother had one of her coughing fits, the Matron simply pulled a disgusted face. "You were right, Mr Jones," she said to the porter. "Nurse, take this one to the infirmary, please. The one on the top floor."

"Thank you, miss," Stella said, genuinely grateful. She wanted to help the nurse get her mother back on her feet, but the Matron stopped her.

"Nurse and Mr Jones will take it from here, dear. You're coming with me."

"Can't I stay with my mother? Please? She's very ill and she–"

"You're not a babe anymore, little girl. Family ties cease to exist once you step through the door of the workhouse, in case you hadn't heard."

"But I could–"

The Matron smacked Stella over the head. "Lesson number two, dear: in the workhouse you do as you're told. Always. No ifs and no buts. Do you understand?"

"Yes, miss."

"Good. Now follow me and I'll give you a clean uniform."

"I don't get to keep my own clothes?"

"The only thing you get to keep in the workhouse is your name, Miss–?"

"Reed. Stella Reed, miss."

"A word of advice, Miss Reed. Whatever your life was like before, it's over. You're a workhouse waif now, just another face among hundreds of others. The sooner you accept that, the sooner you can stop making things harder for yourself."

"Yes, miss."

As she followed the Matron, Stella cast one last glance over her shoulder, in the direction her mother had been taken.

"Do you think my mother will be all right though, miss?"

"Perhaps," the Matron shrugged. "Miracles happen after all. But I've seen people die who weren't half as ill as your mother."

Chapter Two

Stella lay on her back, awake and unable to sleep. Despite being surrounded by dozens of girls of all ages, she felt her only companions in the dormitory were the darkness and the cold. Those, and her constant thoughts of her mother. Nobody told her anything about how her mother was doing, or if she was getting any better at all. And after five days in the workhouse, she wasn't even sure anymore if her mother was still alive.

She assumed someone would at least tell her if her mother passed away. But then again, she was beginning to wonder if anyone would actually bother. Compassion didn't seem to be a quality of the few people she had encountered so far.

If Sarah Reed died, somewhere up there in the infirmary, would someone go through the trouble of enquiring if perhaps the woman had any relatives in the workhouse?

Suddenly, Stella got the irresistible urge to simply get out of bed and find her mother. Now.

She listened to the sounds around her. All she heard was the quiet silence of children sleeping. And she heard the slow breaths of the two girls with whom she shared a bed. They were snuggled up together on the other side of the narrow bed, which wasn't much more than a wooden box with some thin blankets. Stella thought she would be able to get up without disturbing them. She simply had to, if she wanted to see her mother.

Before it was too late.

She had of course asked to see her mother, as recently as the day before even. But Matron had refused each and every time, and Stella had the impression the woman was running out of patience with her.

No, if she wanted to have a chance to see her mother again, she would need to do it in secret. And in a place like the workhouse, where all hours of the day were scheduled and planned for her, that meant she would have to do it now, before the others woke up.

Cautiously, she got out of bed. The boards creaked underneath the shifting weight, and she held her breath. In the darkness of the night, the sound had seemed frightfully loud to her.

But nobody stirred, so she continued on her mission. In the corridor, she kept to the wall and felt her way to the main staircase. All she knew was what she had overheard when they were admitted to the workhouse. Matron had told the nurse to take her mother to the infirmary on the top floor. So Stella thought it made sense to go up the stairs. Hopefully, they would lead to the infirmary where she would find her mother.

If Mother was still alive.

A few times, she hid in the shadows when she was afraid she heard footsteps. But sounds and echoes travelled far and strange in the vast workhouse, and she eventually managed to arrive on the correct floor without being detected.

A cold draught gave her goosebumps underneath her simple nightshift. This close under the roof, she could hear the howling wind outside. Would there really be an infirmary here? It hardly seemed like a suitable location to her.

But when another current of cold air carried the smell of disease and antiseptic, she knew she was in the right place.

Pressing on, she soon found herself in front of an open doorway. Beyond it, she saw a double row of beds. And her instincts told her that she would find her mother in one of them.

None of the nurses seemed to be around, so Stella slipped into the ward and silently moved past the beds. But in the darkness, all the figures lying in the beds looked the same to her. Some were sleeping, others were restless or moaning in their agony. All seemed equally miserable to her. Which one was her mother?

Having come this close, she couldn't give up. So she started calling out with a soft whispering voice. "Mother? Mother, are you here?"

She hurried past a few more beds and continued to whisper, hoping her mother would hear her... and would still be able to recognise her voice.

"Stella?"

The voice that called back sounded frail, broken.

"Mother, where are you?"

"Stella, is that you?"

Having spotted the bed where the voice had come from, she rushed over and searched for her mother's hands lying on top of the covers. They felt cold to the touch, and frighteningly weak.

"Mother, I've found you," she sighed, as she pressed those hands to her face and kissed them.

"Stella, how did you get here?" When her mother spoke, the words came out slowly and in a laboured manner. Talking was clearly a struggle to her, but Stella was ecstatic.

"I had to find you, Mother. Matron didn't want to let me visit you. And no one was telling me anything."

"You'll get into trouble if they find out, darling."

"But I wanted to see you. I simply had to. Are you feeling any better? Your hands are so cold, Mother. You'll pull through, won't you? Like I did?"

"I... don't know, sweetheart."

"But you must! Please? And then maybe we can leave the workhouse. Oh, this is truly an awful place, Mother. Matron said I wasn't allowed to see you, because in the workhouse people stop being family. Please tell me you will get better soon, so you and I can be together again?"

"Hush, my little darling. You're babbling, and I'm... tired."

"I'm sorry, Mother. I'll be quiet. If I promise to be good, can I stay here with you? For a little while? Perhaps I could take care of you, and give you your meals. Instead of the nurse. Maybe that way, you will get better more quickly."

"You're sweet, Stella. But..."

"But what?"

"I don't think I will be getting any better, darling."

"No," Stella shook her head, refusing to believe it. "You only feel that way because you're unwell right now."

"I wish that were true, my angel. But I heard the doctor. Talking to the nurse. I'm dying."

"But you can't." She started crying. "If you die, I shall be all alone in this world. You are the only family I've got left, Mother. You mustn't die. Please don't. Please don't leave me behind."

"It's not my decision to make, angel. Stella, listen to me."

Willing herself to be brave for her mother, she wiped off her tears on her shoulder.

"When I am gone," her mother croaked, "you need to make friends with good people. Loyal friends are just as valuable as family. Sometimes even more."

"But I don't want friends. I want you. I want us to be a family again. So you can't die, Mother." She squeezed her mother's hands as tightly as she dared, and shook her a little.

"I love you, Stella."

"I love you too. Please don't die."

"What's all this noise?" a harsh voice suddenly sounded, as one of the nurses came rushing into the ward, carrying a candle. "You're not supposed to be here!"

"She's my mother, and I wanted to see her," Stella whimpered.

But the nurse grabbed her by the arm and pulled her away from the bed.

"These people are very sick and they need their rest." She shoved Stella in the direction of the door. "And little girls like you need their sleep. So get back to your dormitory this very instance, or I shall call Matron."

"Please let me stay by my mother's side, miss. I could–"

"Go! Matron shall be very cross if we wake her up at night. Do you want to make her angry?"

"No, miss."

"Then get back to bed."

Defeated, and hugging herself against the terrifying cold in her heart, Stella made her way back to her dormitory and crawled into bed. She didn't think she would be able to sleep, but in the morning she gave a start when Matron herself woke her up.

Fearing she had overslept, she jumped up. All around her however, the other girls were only just beginning to stir. So why had Matron come to personally wake her up?

"Miss Reed, your mother passed away last night. Here's her hairbrush. She won't be needing it anymore, and I'm sure she would have liked you to have it. It's a nice brush."

Stella didn't know what to say. Her mother was dead. She was well and truly alone in the world now.

"Wash up," Matron said. "Breakfast is in half an hour."

Chapter Three

The short breaks and idle moments in between their duties were the worst in the workhouse. During most of the day, their activities were well regulated and their instructions clear. They knew exactly where they had to go, when they needed to be there, and what was required of them. Whether it was class with Miss Johnson, picking oakum, doing the laundry or helping in the kitchen, their schedule told them precisely what they were supposed to do.

But occasionally, they had a bit of spare time on their hands. And Stella dreaded those moments.

Although she welcomed the brief respite from the hard work that was demanded of them, she feared the terror that often filled these lulls.

Because no matter how hard she tried over the years, and no matter how good she became at making herself invisible in the shadows, they still managed to find her: the workhouse bullies.

Gliding silently from the laundry house to the classroom in the main building, she hoped she would escape them this time.

Please Lord, just this once?

She had put off leaving the laundry house for as long as she could, pretending to have dropped something so she could hide behind the large washing tubs for a bit. If she gave the others enough of a head start, they might get caught up in their coarse and silly games along the way and forget about her.

So far, her luck was holding out. She didn't see any of the usual mischief-makers in the courtyard she was crossing.

With her heart pounding in her chest, she approached the large double doors that would take her into the main building. She looked through the grimy glass window panes to check the path ahead, and then pulled the door open. All seemed clear.

Not very far to the classroom now, she told herself, increasingly hopeful.

Once she got to the classroom, she knew she would be safe for the duration of their lesson.

Miss Johnson didn't tolerate any bullying or pestering.

Stella liked Miss Johnson. Their teacher was one of the precious few people in the workhouse who were genuinely nice.

And those fond feelings seemed to be entirely mutual. Because Miss Johnson didn't hide her appreciation for the best pupil in her class. Which unfortunately, only added fuel to the hatred of her bullies, who didn't care about reading or being able to write their numbers and letters.

"There she is!"

Stella's feet froze, and her heart sank. They had found her. Running away now was useless she knew. So she stood and waited while they came dashing over to her, whooping and howling like a deranged pack of hungry wolves.

"So you thought you could escape us, did you?" one of them sneered.

"Very clever staying behind in the laundry house like that," another one taunted.

"Didn't do you much good though, did it?"

"You know we always manage to track you down, Your Highness."

The pack laughed, thinking themselves very witty for calling her that.

"Yeah, you're not that clever after all. Not when it comes to the stuff that really matters."

"The only way Stella Reed will ever learn is if they write a book about it."

"Maybe she could write it herself. In that pretty handwriting of hers. 'My Life In the Workhouse: How I Got Beaten Up Again and Again and Again' by Stella Reed."

She let them have their malicious fun. There was no use in replying or trying to outwit them. Talking back only made the inevitable beating worse.

She knew, because she had tried often enough.

In the beginning, she had hoped the abuse and the bullying would improve as she grew older. But her tormentors got bigger and stronger as well obviously, and they never failed to attract other newcomers of their ilk.

And so she found herself in that familiar predicament once more: surrounded by a group of boys and girls who took a savage delight in taunting her, while she waited for the inevitable.

"What's the matter, Your Highness? Lost your tongue?"

"Did breakfast displease you this morning, my Lady?"

"Maybe she doesn't want to talk to us because she feels we're beneath her."

"Is that it, Stella? Do you think you're better than us?"

Someone gave her a shove, hoping to provoke her. That was usually how the bullying turned more violent. And it was no different this time.

They shoved and pushed her between them, as if she were a ball or a rag doll caught up in a rough game. When someone stuck out their foot, Stella tripped and fell. Knowing what came next, she pulled up her legs and tried to cover her head with her arms. It didn't protect her from their blows, but it was better than lying on the floor completely defenceless.

Fists and feet started to rain down on her, while their screams became increasingly frantic and unhinged.

"What's all this racket?" the voice of Miss Johnson shouted from somewhere further down the corridor. "You lot, stop that right now!"

Stella's attackers scattered, defiantly yelling a few more insults at her. To them, this was merely an interruption. They would continue their fun at the first opportunity they got.

Miss Johnson hurried over to where Stella was still lying on the floor. "You poor girl," she said. "Can you stand up?"

With a painful moan, Stella sat upright. "I'll be fine, miss. They've done far worse than this."

"I'm so sorry, Stella. It's my fault. I should have been waiting for you outside the classroom. Then this wouldn't have happened."

"You're not to blame, miss. They probably would have been waiting for me elsewhere."

"Still..." The young teacher bit her lip, frustrated at the injustice that went unpunished and at her inability to do anything about it. "Shall we get you on your feet?"

Leaning on Miss Johnson, she slowly got back up.

"You are such a brave girl, Stella."

"I have no other choice, miss." She winced at the pain in her side. One of her assailants had hit her pretty bad there. "Miss?"

"Yes, Stella?"

"Why do people do this to each other?"

Miss Johnson sighed. "I think it's mainly out of a twisted kind of envy. You're the sort of person they would secretly like to be. But since they can't be you, they get mad."

"Will it ever stop, miss?"

The teacher gave her a careful hug. "One day it will, dear. One day, you will leave this workhouse and build a life of your own. And there won't be any bullies or nasty people to hurt you."

"I hope so."

"Oh, all this unpleasantness nearly made me forget. The Master wants to see you in his office."

"Why? What is it about?" Immediately, Stella was apprehensive. Being called into the Master's office usually wasn't good news. She had never been sent there before, but she had heard others tell frightening tales of what happened.

"I don't know," Miss Johnson replied. "He didn't say." The kind teacher smiled and put a reassuring hand on her shoulder. "Let's just go and wash your face and hands, so you look your best."

Stella nodded. Whatever the reason why the Master wanted to see her, she would stand in front of him without showing any fear. Just like she did with her bullies.

Chapter Four

Her body still smarting from the assault, Stella took a deep breath before she knocked on the Master's door. The smell of old wood and dust mingled with the aroma of fresh tea as she entered the office.

"Ah, there she is," the Master said. "Come closer, girl, so Mrs Bosworth can have a look at you."

Stella nodded, and did as she was told. In front of his great wooden desk, a lady of forty had taken a seat. While a set of squinting blue-grey eyes looked her up and down, Stella too took the opportunity to examine the woman. Her hair was styled in a manner that betrayed the employment of a lady's maid, as did her clothing. Around her waist, layers of dark green fabric covered the chair she was sitting on.

"She looks well fed," Mrs Bosworth commented. "Not particularly strong, but she should suffice for household duties."

Ah, so that's why she was wanted in the Master's office, Stella understood immediately. The workhouse had found her a potential employer! She knew most of the children were sent away at some point, to work as servants, apprentices or labourers. Lately, she had often wondered when her turn would come. And what her chosen fate would be.

Now it seemed she was to become a maid. And for a wealthy family from the looks of it.

"I assume the girl has been taught the ways of housekeeping?"

Mrs Bosworth's voice was artificially nasal, and Stella wondered if she always talked like that, or if the lady merely wanted to block out the stench of the part of the city she had ventured into. But even without that annoying tone, Stella noticed there wasn't any trace of warmth in the woman's speech.

"Absolutely, Mrs Bosworth," the Master answered. "She can clean, serve food and sew. She also knows her way around the written word."

The latter he said with an air of pride, as if it was his own accomplishment.

"I'm employing a maid, not entertaining a literary circle," the lady replied. "Her duties will be to obey my commands, and those will be given verbally. Reading is an idle pastime not suitable for a maid."

"Of course, Mrs Bosworth. You will be pleased to hear that Stella is one of, if not *the* best girl we have. She has never uttered a single word of insolence, and she is very swift in her work, indeed. At fourteen years of age, she is a fine young girl. And quite polite too, aren't you, Stella?"

"Yes, sir," Stella said. "I'll be glad to be of service to you, ma'am."

For another moment, Mrs Bosworth's cold gaze lay upon Stella, almost as if she wished to determine whether the girl's heart was as pure as her words.

But no one could see behind Stella's courteous expression once it had taken over her face. In a place like this, you learned to hide your true emotions from those who would take advantage of them.

What neither the Master nor the lady in green could see was the excitement that filled

Stella's heart. Since arriving on the steps of the workhouse so many years ago, she had dreamt of being taken in by a kind mistress.

The life of a maid was no doubt a hard one. But it couldn't be any worse than scrubbing the floors of the place where her mother had died, and where Stella herself was mocked and beaten virtually every day.

She watched Mrs Bosworth as the lady continued the conversation with the Master. Her hands were neatly folded in her lap, and there was a golden wedding ring on her left hand. Her nose was sharp and straight, but apart from that, her face told the tale of faded beauty. Her greying hair must have been blonde many years ago.

Despite the civilised appearances, Stella decided her new mistress was not kind. But that conclusion could hardly stifle her joy, for she dreamed of the grand house the Bosworth family were bound to live in. A place with portraits on the wall, and splendid gardens – like in the Jane Austen stories she loved to devour when she could get her hands on them.

Maybe finally, after spending much of her young life in a place so devoid of warmth and laughter, she could finally be surrounded by nice people again.

"Just to make one thing abundantly clear," Mrs Bosworth said to the Master. "She is to follow orders and dedicate herself exclusively to her work. No taking a fancy to any of the boys in my staff. We had enough of that with the last one."

She rolled her eyes to stress her annoyance, and the Master duly responded by tutting along softly.

"I expect my maids to perform their duties adequately. And if this girl's work is not to my liking, then she will be back here in an instant."

"I understand completely, Mrs Bosworth. I am familiar with the sort you are alluding to. Causes nothing but trouble. And with our pickings from the street, I'm afraid we do not always get the best boys and girls. But I can assure you that Stella is of an altogether different nature. She used to be from a decent household, before the family sadly fell on hard times. She won't give you any trouble."

"I should hope not. And this is exactly why I insisted on seeing her first. So I could judge for myself if she was a suitable candidate."

"That is very wise of you, Mrs Bosworth. As soon as you entered my office, I could tell you were an expert judge of character."

Accepting his obvious attempt at flattery, Mrs Bosworth nodded.

"Very well then, I suppose she will have to do. Let's discuss your fee. As for you," –she turned to Stella– "You are coming with me. My housekeeper shall instruct you on all that is expected of you. Do you understand?"

"Yes, my Lady."

"Go pack your things and report back," the Master said. "With haste."

"Yes, sir. Thank you, ma'am."

Leaving the two grown-ups to haggle over the money, Stella quickly disappeared from the office. And there was even a noticeable bounce to her step, as she hurried to the children's dormitory.

She almost didn't notice the others whispering to each other, wondering what might have happened in the master's office to make the girl so happy. She had got used to tuning out their laughter, so she just went on her merry way. She didn't have much to pack, only the hairbrush that had belonged to her mother, and a well-thumbed penny novel Miss Johnson had given her last year, as a reward for her commitment in class.

Holding her few possessions close to her, Stella took a moment for one last look around the room. Never again would she have to wake up between the damp cold stone walls of Bethnal Green workhouse, freezing to the bone the moment she left the warm covers of the bed.

And never again would somebody mock her for her talents or for being who she was. She would become a real maid, earn a proper wage and have a clean roof over her head.

Suddenly she had to think of her family and the house they used to live in. It had been by no means grand, but they had called it home. Stella still remembered the smell of the biscuits her mother used to bake whenever they had the money for such treats.

Thinking of her mother made her sad. But then she pushed the feeling aside, straightened her back and whispered, "I will find a good home and have my own family one day, Mother. I promise. Even if I have to work really hard for it. Leaving this horrible workhouse is only the first step."

Chapter Five

The next morning, Stella hadn't been in the breakfast room for more than fifteen minutes when she got her first proper taste of Mrs Bosworth's character and temperament.

Used to the rough and simple skirts of the workhouse uniform, she moved slowly and carefully in her freshly pressed, long black servant's dress.

Too slowly to Mrs Bosworth's liking, it appeared.

"Don't dawdle, girl," the lady of the house nagged. Instead of eating her breakfast, she watched Stella's every move.

Nervous about making a mistake, Stella began to sweat under the different layers of clothing. And she had to keep herself from scratching at the unfamiliar cap on her head. Still, she managed to fill her mistress' cup without spilling even a single drop of tea.

The more experienced servants were busy serving food and keeping the table tidy. Being the new girl, Stella had been told to limit herself to pouring tea, and to learn by keeping her eyes and ears open. And for the rest, she was to stand out of the way and wait for further instructions.

So that's exactly what she did. She stood, she waited, and she observed.

She got ample opportunity to study the personalities and the dynamics of the Bosworth family as well.

On the opposite end of the long mahogany table sat Mr Bosworth. A man of fifty, who put three heaped spoons of sugar in each of his cups of tea, and whose head was losing the last few tufts of hair he had left.

Next to him sat his young son Alfred. Stella guessed the boy was only a little bit younger than herself. He had his father's chubby cheeks but his mother's golden hair, which had been cropped short and combed to the sides with an oily wax.

"How is the French coming along, Alfie?" Mrs Bosworth enquired, after swallowing a piece of her quail egg.

"Oh, I've made good progress, Mother. Mr Dumont says I should soon be able to have proper conversations in French."

The boy seemed proud, smiling to himself as he dabbed his mouth with his napkin.

"Very good. Mr and Mrs Cowden will call on us later today. And as they have just returned from a trip to France, I would be pleased if you entertained us with your skill in the language."

"But Mother," Alfie objected. "I was planning to take Atlantis out for a ride in the park. Father promised I could!"

As he spoke, his voice grew more disappointed. This had not been the first time his mother upset his plans, Stella figured.

"Nonsense," Mrs Bosworth replied. "Reginald has said no such thing, have you, dear?" She shot her husband a strict look that tolerated no contradiction.

"Of course not, Josephine," the master of the house said, not even looking up from his plate.

Alfie looked like he couldn't believe his own ears.

"There you have it," Mrs Bosworth said, almost triumphantly. "You can ride your horse

36

another time. Today I want you to make a good impression on our guests. I want them to see what a fine young man you are. But they have no chance of seeing that, if you are out riding Lord knows where on that smelly beast every day."

"Atlantis isn't smelly," Alfie argued vehemently. "Pete brushes him every day and rubs him down after every ride."

The glare his mother directed at him quickly made him keep his tongue and stare at his plate instead.

Shamed into submission, Stella thought.

"You are to discuss your plans with me, Alfie," Mrs Bosworth spoke. "Always. Is that understood?"

Alfie's voice sounded meek. "Yes, Mother."

"As for you, Emma," the lady barked in Stella's direction. Mrs Bosworth refused to call her maids by their real names. They were all either Marys or Emmas. A practice that made it hard for Stella to know when she herself was being spoken to.

"You have a pair of perfectly good eyes, I presume?"

"Yes, ma'am?"

"Then use them, and fill up our cups when they are empty. I trust we needn't call for you every time?"

"No, ma'am," Stella said and hurried to pour more tea into her mistress' china cup.

As she went round the table, Alfie gave her an apologetic smile. Stella nodded, careful not to show too much emotion. It was forbidden for servants to interact with the family members any more than strictly necessary. The boy seemed to have a different opinion on the matter.

"Thank you, but I've had enough tea," he said. "Could you pass me the butter over there though, if you don't mind?"

"Alfred, dear," Mrs Bosworth huffed. "It needn't concern you what Emma does or doesn't mind. We don't pay her for her to stand around."

The sideways glance she threw in Stella's direction showed nothing but contempt.

"Yes, Mother." Alfie let his head sink again.

Poor boy, Stella thought. She didn't remember her own mother to be like that. No, her mother had always been kind, and she had never so much as raised her voice. This first breakfast with the Bosworths made Stella miss her old family life again.

"Reginald, would you please close your mouth while you're chewing. The scullery maid has better manners than you!"

Mrs Bosworth's harsh remarks seemed to bounce off the walls and fill the entire room with cold unpleasantness. Her husband hastily closed his mouth and, almost instinctively, pulled in his head as if he was a tortoise seeking protection within its shell. The move had the unwanted comical effect of multiplying the number of his chins. He mumbled a few words of apology to his wife, but kept silent otherwise.

Stella's prior excitement about her new life began to wane with every word that left the thin-lipped mouth of Mrs Bosworth.

At the workhouse, the children mocked and bullied her, that much was true. But there, she had at least enjoyed the reputation of being smarter and perhaps even somewhat superior to the others. Here she was "Emma" – nothing more than another servant girl in black frocks and white aprons. Here, she was nobody.

As the family breakfast dragged on however, she soon learned that it wasn't just the servants who suffered under the cruel lashes of the lady's venomous tongue. Stella was not proud of the tiny spark of glee that crossed her mind every time she heard her mistress speak ill of their relatives and many acquaintances, but it felt good to have the negative attention lifted off her own shoulders for a change.

So it's not just me then, she sighed with relief. No one was safe from the brutal judgement of Mrs Bosworth, it seemed. The woman was a veritable vessel of disdain and loathing.

Stella couldn't help but pity young Alfie and his father though. The two Bosworth men appeared friendly and docile enough.

Standing close to the wall, careful not to lean against it of course and always maintaining a watchful eye on everyone's teacup, she noticed the boy kept looking at her whenever his mother was too busy chattering and complaining about this or that person.

At first, his stares made her feel uncomfortable. She had read enough romance stories to know that wealthy men would often foster unwholesome desires towards their female staff. But the more she observed young Alfie Bosworth, the less she believed he would be inclined to harbour such feelings.

No, his gaze appeared to be nothing but friendly. It was the way a lonely child looked at a potential companion. And she knew what that felt like. At the workhouse, she too had often longed to have a best friend. Or any old friend for that matter.

Sorry, Alfie, she thought. *But I don't think your dear mother would approve of you being friends with the maid.*

Chapter Six

The splendour of the Bosworth residence didn't extend to the servants' quarters naturally. Where lavishly expensive wallpaper adorned the walls of the family dining room, blank and damp walls surrounded Stella as she ate her supper with the other household staff.

She didn't mind. She had been up since sunrise, and her legs ached from standing and running all day. These few minutes of rest felt like a blessing to her exhausted body.

While she hungrily ate her stew, the smell of fresh cake filled the room. But she was disappointed to find out only the more senior servants would get their hands on the sugary treat. Here, at the lower servants' table, she recognised a few familiar faces from breakfast.

Next to her sat the other housemaids, Lily and Margaret, as well as the young scullery maid Esther. But this evening, there were more people present whom she hadn't met yet. Among them, two boys on the bench opposite her. The one sitting directly across from her was the first to catch her eye. Looking perhaps two years older than her, he was busy spooning away at his stew like every other young member of the household staff.

Stella glanced at him shyly while he appeared to be focussed on his supper. Dark brown curls framed his face. He was rather handsome. The other boy not so much. That one's face seemed crude by comparison. His hands were rough, and when he spoke, he revealed a few missing teeth.

It was the curly-haired one who broke the silence that hung over their table like a heavy blanket.

"You're the new girl, aren't you?"

His dark brown eyes fixated her curiously.

Stella nodded.

While chewing, he looked her up and down.

"You look like an Emma to me. Doesn't she, Tommy?" he said, turning to the boy next to him.

Tommy shrugged.

"If the hag calls her Emma, I get your apple," the first boy smiled confidently, and shook on it with his friend.

"She does," Stella replied in surprise.

Tommy groaned and rolled his eyes. "How did you know?" he asked the first boy.

"I wouldn't be winning your apples every time a new maid joined the house if I told you my secret, now would I?" he said cheekily, as he quickly pinched Tommy's apple and took a bite from it.

"What's your real name then?" he asked, turning towards her again.

"Stella," she said with a smile.

"Nice to meet you, Stella. My name's Pete. Has your first day been all right?"

Stella thought about his question for a moment. She didn't want to seem like she was complaining, so she said, "More or less. Everything's still new and I make plenty of mistakes."

"You'll learn quickly. You seem bright enough," Pete said, and gave her a broad smile. "Mrs Bosworth will haunt you in your dreams, but during the daytime, thankfully, she's busy a lot."

Stella chuckled. "I wonder if she ever gets tired of bossing everyone around. Why bother having servants if you can't let them do their work?"

Pete shrugged. "Who knows. I thank the good Lord every day that she doesn't come to the stables personally. Makes life easier."

"So, you're a stable boy then?" Stella asked. The question was purely for conversation's sake, since Pete's intense smell of horses had already given away his occupation before he even sat down.

"Like my father was when he was my age. When I'm older, I hope to become a head coachman like him."

He nodded his head in the direction of a man at the other table, who did indeed bear a striking resemblance to him. Stella could tell from the gleam in Pete's eye that he was fond of his father and their profession.

"But right now, I'm just taking care of the horses. Including Alfie's of course. They've got quite a lot of horses, the Bosworths. So it's hard work. But I'd rather clean stable boxes all day than have Lady Meanworth watch my every move."

He took a moment to look at Stella again.

"I'm rambling. Where did you come from so suddenly, anyway?"

"The workhouse." She did not need to elaborate on that. Her background was a common one among the people she worked with.

Pete nodded silently.

Then, after a thoughtful pause, he asked, "Anything entertaining happen while you were working today?"

It was an obvious attempt to steer the conversation onto lighter topics. But Stella seized upon it gladly.

"Well, I wouldn't call it entertaining maybe. But it did make me giggle, secretly."

"Go on then," he encouraged her. "I do like a good giggle myself."

"They had guests today," Stella began. "And there was this little girl of five or six years old. And she kept saying the rudest things. Like how the hallway had smelled funny, the tea tasted too strong again, and that the curtains were of poor taste."

She chuckled at the memory.

"Everyone knew that she had probably picked up those comments from her mother, but nobody dared say anything. They just blushed like the trees in autumn, and I had to force myself not to grin. You could tell Mrs Bosworth was fuming."

"Serves her right," Pete said chuckling. "She's been making our lives a living hell ever since she was born."

"Ever since she was born?" Stella laughed. "You don't think she came into this world sniping and criticising, do you?"

Several of the others at the table snorted, clearly sharing the same idea about their mistress.

His nose turned up, Pete pulled an arrogant face to imitate Mrs Bosworth. "Oh Mama," he spoke with a squeaky, nasal voice. "This fine bed linen is much too crude for me. I simply must have silk sheets."

Everyone at their table laughed at his excellent little parody.

"Mind that tongue of yours, young Mr Draper," a strict voice sounded from the other side of the room. It was Mrs Burch, the housekeeper. "Or one day your jokes will land you into trouble."

Pete's father looked up from his supper too, but only briefly. His expression had seemed perfectly neutral to Stella, and she gathered the man felt there wasn't anything he needed to add to Mrs Burch's warning.

Once everyone had turned their attention back to their own plate, Stella and Pete kept exchanging knowing glances. Like they were accomplices in some secret plot now. Stella noticed she was feeling lighter than before.

They didn't have a chance to continue their conversation, as supper was finished soon after, and it was time for everyone to return to their duties again.

Stella noticed a slight sting of disappointment in her chest. She would have no one to talk to all evening, and the little taste of normality that Pete had given her would be terribly missed. But just as she and the other maids started to clear the tables, Pete suddenly appeared by her side.

"Listen, Stella," he whispered casually. "You seem like a nice girl. Come and visit me in the stables whenever you like. Might help you to clear your head and let off some steam."

And with a wink, he added, "Over there we can poke fun at Mrs Meanworth as much as we like."

"Well, if you put it like that," she giggled, "I have no choice but to come and see you."

She was old and wise enough to know boys sometimes wanted more than friendship or innocent fun from girls. But Pete didn't seem like that sort of boy to her.

"Good," he grinned happily. "Don't wait too long."

When he gave her another one of his bright smiles, Stella couldn't resist smiling back at him. He turned round, and she followed him with her eyes until he had left the kitchen.

Suddenly nervous that someone had seen her staring at him, she cleared her throat and quickly resumed with her task of stacking dirty plates and cutlery.

All throughout the evening and right until she went to bed hours later, thoughts of Pete occupied her mind. After having spent just a few minutes laughing, her work seemed more bearable.

Pete had done that for her.

And so she resolved to visit him in the stables as soon as she had a few moments of free time. If needed, she would work extra hard in order to have a bit more spare time.

Chapter Seven

"Enter," Mr Bosworth's voice sounded after Stella knocked a second time. She had grown used to being patient with the master of the house, as his mind always seemed to be miles away from his body.

Today however, she found out what distracted him so much. Entering his impressive study, she couldn't help but look around in awe, and a little disgust. On all four walls of the room, dozens upon dozens of dead butterflies were mounted in wooden frames protected by glass casing.

As Stella crossed Mr Bosworth's study to get to his desk with her tray of tea and cake, she glanced at the spectacular displays of colourful insects, pinned next to each other like badges. Mrs Bosworth hated it when she lingered, but her husband didn't appear to mind. In fact, he barely registered her presence. He sat at his desk, intently studying the pages of several books thicker than Stella's fist.

"I have brought you tea and cake, sir. Where shall I put down the tray?"

No response. She decided to set it down on the coffee table next to the sofa, which was the only surface in the room without books on it.

Stella smiled to herself. If she had the means of Mr Bosworth, her own room wouldn't look much different. She knew all too well the joy of losing herself in a good book, and the welcome distraction it offered when the real world seemed unbearable.

Would all his books be about butterflies though? What a bizarre thing to be fascinated by, she thought to herself.

"I have placed your tea and cake on this table, sir," she informed him politely.

He looked up briefly, slightly confused as if he only now realised there was someone else in the room with him. "Did you say cake?"

Stifling the urge to laugh, she politely replied, "Yes, sir. It's right here. Unless you want me to bring it over to your desk?"

He seemed shocked at the thought of food and drink coming too close to his precious books. "No, over there will do nicely. I'll have a quick bite in a moment."

She bobbed a short curtsy and left the study. When she had closed the door softly, she was startled by someone standing next to the door in the gloomy corridor.

"I'm sorry," Alfie said. "I didn't mean to frighten you." He shifted his weight uncomfortably from one foot to the other.

"It's all right, sir. I just didn't expect you to be standing there, that's all."

She stood with her head slightly bowed, awaiting his permission to be on her way.

"Was it your first time in there?" he asked, nodding towards the door.

"Yes, it was, sir. I just brought your father some refreshments."

Although Alfie had been kind to her since her arrival a week ago, she was still careful around him. The other servants spoke ill of him.

"Something isn't right with that one," the other stable boy Tommy had said once. "The father's got the spine of a slug, and the mother kicks the both of them around like the rest of us.

So he tries to play with us like we're his pets. Until he grows tired of us, I'm sure."

"Oh Tommy, let the boy be," Pete had said. "He's a lonely little lad with a serpent for a mother and a limp fish for a father. Honestly, if we're the best company he has, we should be flattered."

"Oh, I bet you're flattered," Tommy had rebutted. "You're master Alfred's most favourite pet of all."

His comment had made the table laugh, and Pete had playfully slapped his friend on the back of the head, grinning broadly himself.

Remembering Pete's words from that evening put a smile on Stella's face.

"Don't worry if he doesn't talk to you," Alfie said, pulling her back to the present. "He doesn't talk much to me either. I don't think there has ever been a day when he wasn't in his study."

Although the tone of his voice was casual, Stella noticed the sadness in his eyes.

"Your name is Stella, right?" he asked.

When he saw the surprised look on her face, he added, "Pete told me. He speaks of you a lot."

For some reason that last comment gave her a warm, funny feeling. Pete talked to Alfie about her?

"Speaking of Pete," the boy continued. "He's at the stables right now. Have you had a chance to go there yet?"

She saw his face light up when he mentioned the stables.

"I can't say that I have, no," Stella replied. Every waking moment of her day, she was scurrying around the house, serving food and drinks, preparing rooms, cleaning and tidying, or facing Mrs Bosworth's admonishments. If she was seen resting, either the housekeeper Mrs Burch or the lady of the house herself were sure to get Stella on her feet again quickly.

Taking a stroll to the stables without a clear purpose would have seemed like she was trying to avoid work. And she didn't want to risk falling out of favour with the other servants either. Friendships were scarce in this household. The last thing she needed was more enemies.

"Would you like to come with me to see them?" the boy asked. "Don't worry. If somebody asks, we'll just say I ordered you to escort me."

Stella nodded, excited about the idea of having some free time, even if it was only for a short moment.

"Great," Alfie beamed. "Follow me."

He darted down the stairs with remarkable speed, making Stella nervous his bounding footsteps would draw unwanted attention to them. She also realised she had no idea where exactly the stables were, or how to get to them. So she was surprised when Alfie led her down another flight of stairs.

"Shouldn't we be going outside?" she asked, suddenly fearful he might be playing a childish prank on her.

"There's an underground tunnel that leads to the mews at the back of the house," he explained. "That way, we can get there and stay dry even when it's raining."

Opening the door to the tunnel, he said, a bit sadly, "Although I suspect it may also be to keep the servants from passing through our garden."

Stella nodded. At first, she was hesitant to enter the dark tunnel. It was poorly lit and it smelled of damp. But it would also take her to Pete.

Leading the way, Alfie continued chattering along happily. With every step further through the tunnel, he seemed to come more to life.

"I'm there every day, you know," he said. "To check how Atlantis is doing. He's my favourite horse, you see. And of course, Pete is always there as well. Have you met Pete yet?"

"Yes, I have, sir."

"Please, call me Alfie."

She took a sharp intake of breath. It would be unheard of for a maid to call the son of her master and mistress by his first name.

But he had noticed her reaction. "Seriously, I insist. I want you to call me Alfie. Pete does. Not with my mother or anyone else around obviously. But in the stables and when we're alone, I'm Alfie."

He smiled the friendliest smile at her. "And you're Stella."

The idea still made her feel uneasy. But it was nice to be called Stella and not Emma by at least one member of the Bosworth family.

As soon as they came out of the tunnel and into the stables, the distinct smell of horses filled her nose. Although rather peculiar, she didn't think it was an unpleasant smell. There was something reassuringly warm and comforting about it – just like the place itself.

Stella immediately began to understand why Alfie loved to spend time here.

"Isn't it amazing?" Alfie whispered, taking a deep breath.

She had to agree that it was. Before them lay a short corridor with stable boxes on either side. Standing in those boxes were the prettiest horses she had ever laid eyes on. And in one of the boxes, Stella heard the sound of a pitchfork scraping against the stone floor underneath the straw, and the happy whistling of a tune.

Pete, she knew. It had to be him.

Alfie snapped his fingers suddenly. "I've just remembered," he said, slightly irritated. "Mr Dumont will be arriving any minute now, for my French class. I'd better hurry back. He always yells at me when I'm late."

Stella wanted to turn around as well, and follow him back to the house. But he stopped her and said, "No, you stay here for a while. Ask Pete to show you around. And tell him I said hello."

He threw her one last smile and then disappeared into the tunnel, leaving her alone with the horses... and Pete.

Chapter Eight

One of the stable doors opened, and out stepped Pete. When he saw her, he stopped whistling and a smile appeared on his face.

"Well, well," he said, wiping his hands on a rag dangling from the bottom of his braces. "What a nice surprise to see you here. Where's Alfie? I though I'd heard his voice."

As he came walking over to her, all Stella could see was his beaming smile and his shock of curly hair.

"He just–" She pointed over her shoulder, at the tunnel door behind her, fumbling her words. "But then he–"

She tried to think of something more intelligible to say, but suddenly her mind went blank. Feeling shy and rather self-conscious, she dropped her gaze to her feet.

Her shoes had become dirty from walking through the tunnel, she noticed. *Bother*, she thought. *Now I'll have to clean them first.*

"Alfie doesn't bring servant girls here often," Pete said. "So I suppose you should feel honoured."

He heaved a bag of horse feed onto his shoulders. The sleeves of his sweaty work shirt had been rolled up, exposing his muscular forearms and large hands. As he tilted the bag to pour its contents into the feeding buckets, Stella watched his movements. They seemed almost effortless.

"I will feel less honoured when Mrs Bosworth questions me about my whereabouts," she said. "I'm quite busy."

Pete set down the bag. "And yet you're still here."

A smile crept over his face as he came closer towards her. A few of his curls stuck to his sweaty forehead, and he wiped them away with the back of his hand.

"I'm sorry I can't welcome you to the stables looking more presentable," he quipped, even though he didn't look any different than how Stella knew him.

As he stood in front of her, she noticed how strong his build was. He had broad shoulders and long legs that made him quite a bit taller than her. His brown eyes watched her curiously.

"What are you looking at that is so interesting anyway?" he asked with a grin that meant he knew exactly what she was looking at. Stella felt the heat rush to her cheeks.

"Don't worry," he laughed. "I'm only joking. I'm quite glad you came actually."

"Alfie asked me. He showed me the way. But then he had to run back, to be in time for his class. Oh, and he told me to say hello."

She wished she sounded less like a silly lovestruck maid, and a bit smarter than she just had. But Pete didn't seem to mind.

"That's very kind of him," he replied. "And as I said, welcome. I'm glad you're here. Horses make for wonderful companions, but they lack your charm, quite frankly."

Slowly stroking underneath the long forelock of an extraordinarily beautiful horse, he added with a smile, "Don't tell them that though. It might hurt their feelings."

Stella laughed. "I didn't even know horses had feelings."

"Oh, but they do," Pete said, more seriously. "They're very clever. And they don't need expensive private tutors either."

"That one's gorgeous," she said, indicating the horse he was stroking. Its coat looked shiny with health, a perfect finish to its powerful yet graceful body.

"This is Atlantis, Alfie's favourite."

Despite its impressive size and strength, the animal was completely relaxed, surrendering itself to Pete's friendly touch.

"He's like a giant," Stella admired. "And yet he seems so sweet and docile."

Pete smiled. "Maybe they are afraid of showing what they are capable of, because they don't know how their masters would react."

He gazed at her for a moment, before returning his attention to Atlantis again. "We servants have that in common with them."

She had never thought about their similarities to horses before. It reminded her of what Tommy had said the other day.

"Do you think we're like horses to Alfie?" she blurted out. "Are we just his pets? His playthings until he grows tired of us?"

Pete furrowed his brow. "Don't take Tommy too seriously, Stella. He loves to complain when he's tired, and Alfie is low-hanging fruit for him."

He crossed his arms. "I think Alfie genuinely sees us as friends. As kindred spirits, if you will. Which is all the sadder, because that can never be the case."

Stella nodded. "He speaks very highly of you. Almost as if you were a big brother to him."

Pete sighed. "I wish I could think of him the same way. He's a good boy. He's considerate and smart, but he's not one of us."

He shook his head and slipped Atlantis a treat from his pocket.

"Alfred Bosworth may think of me as a friend, but I have to see him as my master. If I forget to do that, if I get too close, it's me who will suffer the consequences in the end, not him. He can always get another stable boy to talk to when he's bored."

He stepped away from Atlantis and picked up his pitchfork again.

"Me on the other hand, I can't afford such foolish notions. I can't let an imagined friendship make me lose my job and disappoint my father."

Pete's words made Stella's heart sink a little. She understood the gap that existed between their masters and the likes of her. But that didn't make it any easier to swallow. Why was she considered to be less, compared to someone who'd had the good fortune of being born into a rich family?

To change the topic, she asked, "How did you come to work here?"

"My father has worked for the Bosworth family most of his life," Pete answered. "And I started at the stables when my mother died."

Seeing the pitiful look in her eyes, he hastily added, "It was a long time ago. I don't really remember her."

"I remember my mother," she said. "She died when I was little, right after we arrived in the workhouse."

"I'm sorry to hear that," Pete said with a soft voice. "I'm sure she was lovely."

"She was. I've never met a kinder person in my life," Stella said with a heavy heart. "I try to be like her every day. In this house though–"

Her voice trailed off. Why was she sharing this with him? In the stables of all places. She wasn't even supposed to be here!

But something about Pete and the calming presence of the horses made her want to open up and speak of her thoughts and worries.

"In this house," she pressed on, "it's not always easy to be kind. I know it's wrong of me to say this, but sometimes I have half a mind of strangling Mrs Bosworth when she's being so mean to me."

Pete chuckled.

"I can honestly tell you that you're not alone with those thoughts. But meeting anger with kindness is a very powerful thing," he assured her. "And I admire you for it."

"Thank you," she said, lowering her gaze again.

"Seriously," he insisted. "I mean it. As a stable boy, I don't need to deal with Lady Meanworth all that much. You though, you have her breathing down your neck from morning till evening. It takes strength and character to keep smiling in the face of someone as nasty as her."

Stella wasn't used to compliments. At the workhouse, she only got them sparingly, and almost exclusively from Miss Johnson. And at the Bosworths' of course, she stood a better chance of finding a rare pearl in an oyster than of receiving a heartfelt compliment.

But being all alone in the stables with Pete, talking about horses and masters and servants – that made her feel good.

The warmth of the horses around her, and the sincere kindness of Pete, all seemed to thaw something within her that the Bosworth household was trying hard to freeze to death.

Chapter Nine

"I would like to take you out riding today, my dear," the gentleman on the sofa said to Mrs Bosworth. His face was framed by a meticulously groomed beard and a moustache that curled up crisply at the edges. Everything about him, from his vain demeanour to his fashionable clothes, betrayed that this was a man who cared an awful lot about his appearance and the impression he made on others.

When Stella rushed to fill up his empty teacup, she stole a quick glance at her mistress. Because there was a rare sight to behold: a smiling, beaming Mrs Bosworth. And it wasn't one of those infamous mean or sarcastic smiles either. Her mistress seemed genuinely pleased and happy to be in the company of her visitor. She wore her hair a little looser than normal, with elegant curls falling down the back of her head. And instead of being adorned with her usual frown, her face was brightened by a pair of twinkling eyes.

"I would love to go out riding, Charles," Mrs Bosworth exclaimed excitedly. "We have earned ourselves a little time out in the park, wouldn't you say?"

"I would indeed say that we have, yes."

Her guest said it with an undertone that implied more than the words being spoken. Still smiling, he raised his cup to his lips.

Mr Charles Preston was not the first visitor of his kind to call upon the mistress regularly. Stella had been told he was Mrs Bosworth's new music teacher. Strangely enough however, she hadn't yet heard a single note of music coming out of the piano room during any of his visits.

Cook had laughed when Stella pointed out this particular oddity. "Before him, she's had a language teacher, an arts tutor, a literary scholar and many more. That woman must be the most educated lady in London."

Still, the whole affair was a strange thing to witness. While Mr Bosworth seemed to confine himself to his study most of the time, his wife had tea and jolly outings with younger and better-looking men. Did her husband know?

Did he care?

Of course, should Stella dare to openly express her suspicions to anyone, her mistress would have her deposited at the door of the workhouse again in a heartbeat. So she simply accepted it wasn't her place to say anything about it.

"Oh Josephine, I forgot to tell you," Mr Preston said, "I fear I shan't be able to call on you for the next few weeks. Urgent business abroad, you see." He bit his lip guiltily. "Do you think you can bear my absence for that long?"

Mrs Bosworth sighed. "I'm afraid I will have to, if you give me no other choice. Don't stay away for too long though," she teased. "Or you shall have been replaced by the time you return."

She giggled daintily, and Stella had to stop herself from staring too overtly at this rather sickening spectacle.

"You know you can't replace me," Mr Preston replied, grinning cheekily. "I'd argue you would have a hard time finding someone..." –he paused briefly to seek the right words– "suitable for the task at hand. After all, it's a very fine art in this particular case."

She tutted at that, but in good spirit. "Are you accusing me of being hard to please?"

"Not at all, Josephine," he raised his hands. "All I am saying is, it takes a skill like mine that is rarely found in other men."

"I know that to be very true unfortunately," she said with one disapproving eyebrow raised at the memory of past lovers. "So I shall simply have to make do without you, I suppose."

Stella could tell that they were feeling clever, twisting their words just enough to be vague. But anyone listening in for more than a minute would have figured out what they were talking about.

"We've had enough tea, Emma." Mrs Bosworth dismissed her with a quick wave of the hand. "And tell Mr Draper to ready two horses for a ride."

Stella nodded politely and left them to their scandalous banter. Closing the double doors and turning round to go find the coachman, she almost bumped into Alfie, giving her a fright.

"Goodness me," she said as she let out a long breath. Was he always lurking around in the shadows?

"I'm so sorry," Alfie apologised. "I didn't mean to startle you."

"That's all right, sir," she said as she continued on her way.

"Alfie," he reminded her, following her like an excitable puppy dog. "You can call me Alfie, remember?"

Stella glanced around to make sure they were alone.

"Okay. So tell me, Alfie. Were you eavesdropping?"

Every day, she would find him alone somewhere in the house, often in front of closed doors. Sometimes he would be reading, and sometimes he simply sat there, staring dreamily at nothing in particular. Yesterday, she had seen him hanging around near the kitchens, where he had no business of being.

"Don't be mad at me," the boy implored in hushed tones. "I'm trying to be good. But Mother's tutors are always so strange. They have the oddest teaching methods. I don't know what to make of it."

Sweet boy, Stella thought. She couldn't tell him of the suspicions every servant in the household had. Not for fear of breaking his heart, but for fear of him telling his mother.

One day he would be old enough to figure it out for himself.

"I wasn't spying on anyone," Alfie continued. "I was merely walking around because Mother told me to stay in the house today. It has rained too much to go riding, she said. And then I hear them planning to go for a ride themselves! That's not fair, is it, Stella?"

He sounded deeply hurt by the injustice.

"I'm bored out of my mind," he sighed. "I just want someone to talk to."

"What about your tutors? You can talk with them, can't you?"

Every time she thought of Alfie Bosworth's unhappy existence, Stella felt the urge to protect him, like a little brother. Still too weak to fend for himself, she felt he needed someone to take him under their wing.

She began to understand Pete's similar dilemma. Although it was easy enough to sympathise with Alfie, they couldn't afford to ignore the stark reality. They were his servants, and he was their master.

But did the boy see it that way as well, she wondered?

"Talking to my tutors isn't the same thing," Alfie said bitterly. "They only want to talk about my lessons." His shoulders dropped even lower. "They're not interested in me."

Stella's heart bled.

"You can talk to me if you'd like," she said carefully.

Immediately, his eyes lit up with excitement. So she felt she needed to caution him. "I'm busy of course. But we may be able to squeeze in a few words here and there."

"I would like that," Alfie said. "It's always great fun speaking to you. Even though I don't know much about you yet."

Stella thought for a moment. She didn't want to tell him anything too personal.

"I love to read," she said finally, almost automatically. His smile grew even broader.

"Oh, that's splendid news," he cried. "What kind of books then?"

"Jane Austen," she said instantaneously. "But it has been forever since I last got my hands on one."

"We have loads of books in our library," Alfie replied, rubbing his chin in thought. "There are bound to be a few titles there that you would like. I'll fetch you some."

"You shouldn't," Stella objected. "I don't have the time anyway, and I wouldn't want your family to think their books went missing."

"Please," Alfie scoffed. "My father only ever reads books about butterflies and biology, and my mother never visits the library. They would never notice."

He thought about his idea for another moment, and then added, "Maybe just don't read them where Mother can see you."

"Of course."

I wouldn't dream of appearing to be idle anywhere near your mother, lad.

She would also have to hide it from the other household staff, she thought. It would look like favouritism, and that would feed the rumour mill. People were already suspicious of her and Pete for engaging with the boy. Word travelled fast along the servants' corridors, and it was hard to restore respectability once it had been lost. Stella didn't have the wealth or social standing of

Mrs Bosworth to protect her from the opinions of other people, so she had to be careful.

But the thought of finally being able to read again filled her with great joy. And if it offered a neglected young boy a moment of escape, then surely, no one should think ill of their secret arrangement?

Chapter Ten

"Take this up to Alfred's room, will you?" Cook said, turning away from Stella as soon as she had placed the tray in her hands. The hurried movement made her skirts swing round her plump legs. Cook was a busy woman, and not keen on wasting time.

It was pure coincidence that Cook had picked her for the task. She just happened to be closest. But Stella was certain Alfie would be pleased with the surprise.

"Your refreshments, sir," she announced solemnly when she entered his room.

He looked up from his books, and instantly, the expression on his face changed from boredom to delight. "Stella," he squealed.

"Shh, not too loud," she said. "The young master isn't supposed to be so happy to see the maid, I think."

But she smiled as she said it, and he covered his mouth with both hands to stifle his giggling laughter.

"Come sit with me for a while," he begged her. "Have some of these biscuits with me. I can't possibly eat them all."

Stella hesitated. She had chores to do. But a few minutes wouldn't hurt anybody, would it? So she sat down on the chair he had pulled up next to him, and took one of the biscuits. Slowly, she bit off a small corner and enjoyed the sweet taste.

"Tell me," Alfie asked, with his mouth full. "What did you think of that last book I gave you?"

"To be frank, I felt the beginning was a tad slow," Stella said. "But after a while I began to like it. You really have to savour every word to understand what the story is all about."

"I completely agree," Alfie nodded emphatically. "I think the full beauty of it only comes to light after reading it multiple times. So much gets lost on you the first time."

He reminded her of his father when he talked like that. She tried to imagine Alfie in a few years, leaning over his desk, analysing books like Reginald Bosworth studied his butterflies.

"I wish I could read it again, Alfie," she sighed. "But I have so much work to do. And I'm usually too tired to read by the time I finally get to bed at night."

"Can't you sneak in a bit of reading time during the day?"

She grinned ruefully at his naive innocence. For all his wealth and privilege, he simply had no idea how hard life was for people like her.

"I'm afraid not," she answered. "And besides, I would feel terribly guilty if I let the others do my work for me, while I was hiding away somewhere to read a book."

Spending time talking to him or Pete was already risky enough. Heaven knows what Mrs Burch would say if the housekeeper caught her reading during work hours.

"I see," Alfie said, somewhat disappointed. While he chomped down on another biscuit, the frown on his face told her he was thinking things over.

"I've got it," he exclaimed suddenly, sending biscuit crumbs flying from his mouth. "I think I have found a solution to your predicament."

"Go on," she humoured him.

"What if I tell Mrs Burch that I require your services for the day? The details shouldn't concern her. All she needs to know is that you are excused for however long I want. And then we can read in the stables, or talk or do whatever we like."

He seemed pleased with himself.

"What do you think?" he asked.

It was a childish idea that would never work. But she couldn't bring herself to tell him that outright.

"It sounds wonderful," she replied instead. "But we need to be very careful. I don't want the others to think you need me for anything improper."

Alfie looked shocked. "I would never," he gasped.

"I know, I know," she said placatingly. "But gossip travels faster than the truth, you should know that. I stand to lose my position if anybody accuses me of improper behaviour."

He wrinkled his forehead in thought.

"We will make sure that won't happen. I could tell Mrs Burch that I need you to carry my supplies."

"Your supplies?"

Thinking his idea through, he got increasingly excited as he improvised.

"I shall tell her I took an interest in outdoor painting, and that I cannot be bothered to carry all the materials and the easel by myself."

"For that to work," she chuckled, "you would have to buy painting supplies. And you'd need to make your mother believe the same story."

Fat chance of that happening.

"Mr Dumont says painting is good for the soul," Alfie said confidently. "So I might just decide to take his recommendation seriously. I would do anything to be able to talk to you in peace, Stella."

"Do you think you could paint me?" she asked, giggling at the idea.

"With my level of expertise, I'm afraid the result would probably look more like a potato than you," he snorted, and they both burst out laughing.

Their laughter died in an instant however, as the door suddenly flew open and Mrs Bosworth swept into the room.

Terrified, Stella jumped to her feet.

The lady of the house was fuming. "You idle little rat," she shrieked while she yanked Stella by the arm. Mrs Bosworth dragged her out of the room with so much force, Stella was afraid she would dislocate her shoulder.

Alfie was on his feet too.

"No, no, no, Mother," he pleaded desperately. "It's a misunderstanding. It was my idea! Do you hear? I invited her. You should punish me, not her."

Without letting go of Stella's arm, Mrs Bosworth whipped round and pointed an angry finger at her son. "Rest assured I am getting to you after I am done with this one!"

She shoved him back inside roughly. "Stay in your room," she growled, and slammed the door shut.

Stella could hear a crying Alfie protesting and whimpering behind the closed door.

"As for you," Mrs Bosworth said as she turned back to Stella. She let the palm of her hand finish the sentence for her. With a loud clap, she slapped her maid hard across the face.

Instinctively, Stella put a hand to her stinging and rapidly reddening face. She felt something warm and moist at the edge of her mouth. When she looked at her hand, there was blood on her fingers.

With her rings, Mrs Bosworth had split Stella's lip.

"Who do you think you are?" the mistress hissed. "You have been a maid in my house for several months. You should know your place by now. Or are you really that thick?"

A vision of crazed fury, Mrs Bosworth was screaming in Stella's face, her hand threatening to lash out again.

"No, ma'am," Stella stammered. "I'm sorry, ma'am."

"You are not to engage in conversation with my son, do you hear?"

"Yes, ma'am," Stella said, meekly staring at the floor.

"If I ever catch you cosying up to Alfred again, I will make sure you'll rot away in that filthy workhouse for the rest of your useless life. Is that understood?"

"Yes, ma'am."

"Now come with me," Mrs Bosworth ordered and half-dragged her down the stairs. "Mrs Burch will know what to do with you."

Stella guessed she would be scrubbing pots and pans in the scullery for a few hours. But that wouldn't be the worst of it. The rumours and whispers of the other staff were likely to be worse than any punishment the housekeeper could come up with.

While Mrs Bosworth marched her to the kitchen, they passed several of the servants, who quickly stood to the side with eyes wide in terror and surprise. Everyone was familiar with the wrath of the lady of the house.

Despite her physical pain and emotional shame, Stella had to think of the mockery she would have to endure at the dinner table tonight.

"Why on earth would you want to chat to a boy like Alfie?" the other maids would ask and snigger.

Stella wouldn't know what to tell them. She just knew that she wanted to make him feel less lonely.

Hours later, when she returned to the room to collect the tray, Alfie was gone. But tucked away underneath the teapot, she found a note.

"*Meet me at the stables after supper,*" it said in his careful handwriting.

That's when Stella knew why she liked the boy. He was one of the only people in this house who would care enough to leave such a note, even after being reprimanded by a vile woman like Mrs Bosworth.

It was dangerous, but Stella decided she would go anyway. She had always thought Alfie was the one who desperately needed a friend. But it wasn't until this moment that she realised just how badly she herself was in need of a friend. Someone who would make this hard life just a little bit more bearable.

And in Pete and Alfie, she had found two of those friends.

Chapter Eleven

Stella watched Pete while he was combing down Alfie's young horse. Atlantis had a beautiful, shiny coat that showed off his elegant build. There was something noble, regal almost, about the gelding.

These horses get more food and better care than most of us servants, Stella thought with a sigh.

But she couldn't bring herself to hate the animals for that. It wasn't their fault the lady of the house was such a mean and cruel woman.

The soft sounds of the brush, and Pete's calm movements put Stella's anxious mind at ease. After supper, she had hesitated to come out here, as she had no desire to be caught by Mrs Bosworth again. But she had decided it was worth the risk, especially since the mistress probably wouldn't dream of coming to the stables.

"She hates the stench," Pete told her. "She expects the horse to be made ready and brought out to her, so she can go out for a ride. And afterwards, she simply hands it back to us – like it's dirty linen or something."

He scoffed and shook his head. "If you ask me, if you're that afraid to have your clothes smell of horses a bit, then you should probably limit yourself to walking. Leave the horses to those who appreciate them, that's what I say."

"I don't think Mrs Bosworth rides for the pleasure of it," Stella said. "It's more of an excuse to go out with her companion."

"I believe you're right," Pete said as he finished brushing Atlantis. He took a step back to admire the result. "Do you know what kind of money I would pay to ride a beauty like this?" he asked, stroking the horse's long neck. "Not that I have any to spare, mind you."

"These people don't realise how lucky they are," Stella smiled dreamily, her thoughts wandering elsewhere.

Somewhere deep down, a memory suddenly popped up in her head. It was a memory of happier times, when she was a little girl and both her parents were still alive. On Sundays, they would go out for a long walk in the park. And on these occasions, her father would sometimes lift her up and carry her on his shoulders. He'd pretend to be a horse and gallup around for a bit, which always made her squeal and giggle with delight.

How perfectly happy and carefree they had been.

But those times were over. And they would never be coming back.

"Hey," Pete whispered, leaning in closer. "Wipe that worried frown off your pretty face, Stella Reed."

She blinked, and snapped out of her daydream. Seeing his smile, she couldn't help but smile back.

"I'm sorry," she said, not entirely sure what she was sorry for.

"Don't be. And don't worry. Mrs Meanworth won't come here."

"Thank you for being a friend, Pete," she said. "I don't know what I'd do without you."

"You'd probably be a maid someplace else. So, if it keeps you around, I'm glad to help." He smiled. "Though I must admit I feel rather guilty."

"Guilty? What for?"

"For being your partner in crime like this," he chuckled. "We might hurt poor Mrs Bosworth's feelings if she found out."

When Stella laughed, she could still feel the sore spot on her cheek where Mrs Bosworth had hit her. But thanks to Pete, her aches and bruises almost became like a badge of honour.

Suddenly, the door to the underground tunnel flew open and an excited Alfie appeared in the stables.

"I'm here at last!" he cried happily. He was out of breath, and Stella guessed he had probably run all the way from the house to the stables.

"Mother wanted to keep me after dinner to recite some poetry to her. I had half a mind of telling her that poetry is the most boring way of telling a story."

"No argument from me on that one," Pete snorted.

Alfie ignored him and instead turned to Stella.

"I wanted to apologise for what happened today. It was careless of me to talk to you in my room, when I am well aware how often my mother just bursts in there."

His blue eyes looked remorseful. With some lone locks sticking up from the pomaded hair and his cheeks red from running, it was hard to be mad at him for long.

"It's all right. You really couldn't have known."

"But I should have," he replied. "I don't want you to get hurt on my behalf. And I wish I could get Mother to stop hitting the servants, but she won't."

Stella studied his face, and he looked genuinely pained about the way his mother treated the staff.

"So from now on," Alfie continued, "you and I will have to be more careful and conduct our conversations in secret. If that's all right with you, of course."

"It is. You're my friend, remember?"

Alfie's face started to glow. "Yes, we're friends," he said, as if he had only just discovered that.

Out of the corner of her eye, Stella noticed Pete's raised eyebrow. Knowing how he felt about the idea of being friends with the son of their masters, she stated, "Down here, we're all friends."

Alfie followed the direction of her gaze. If he understood what was going on, it didn't show on his face.

"Of course," he merely said. "You're both my friends."

"That's nice," Pete replied.

Stella wondered if he was being sarcastic, or if he was simply trying to make light of the situation.

"Do you know what else is nice?" Alfie asked excitedly.

"Freshly baked biscuits?" Pete ventured.

"Well, that too," the boy giggled. "But I was talking about the fact it's going to be summer soon. And that means we will all be moving to the country manor in Buckinghamshire."

The country estate! Stella had heard the other servants talking about it, and the thought of going there filled her with excitement too.

"We all get to go?" she asked.

Alfie nodded. "The entire household. I think only a small handful of the staff stay behind to look after the house. But everybody else moves to the country estate for the summer. The horses too obviously."

"I've never been outside London in my life before," she said. "What's it like in the countryside?"

"You will love it," Alfie assured her. "Life is so much more peaceful and quiet out there. And the air!"

"What about it?" she laughed. "Air is just air, isn't it?"

"Just you wait until you've breathed that countryside air. I swear it will be the purest, freshest thing your nose has ever smelled."

"Like a park in spring, you mean?"

Alfie snorted. "A thousand times better than that!"

Stella turned to Pete, slightly incredulous. She knew the air in London often smelled foul, but surely Alfie was exaggerating?

"It's true," Pete said. "The difference is like night and day."

Stella was intrigued. In her mind, she pictured vast meadows with oceans of pretty flowers bathing in the sunshine. And perhaps there would be a brook nearby, where she could dip her feet into the cool, clear water after work. Every day, she would pick some wildflowers to put in a small jug by her bed. Already, she was beginning to like the idea of these summer stays in the country.

"I'm counting the days until we finally set off," Alfie said. "Over there, I can ride my horse and read books as much as I like. We will have so much fun, Stella."

"*You* will have fun," Pete chuckled. "For us, it's going to be business as usual. Stella will be cleaning rooms and serving tea. And I'll be mucking out stables. Just like here."

He was right, Stella knew. And it reaffirmed to her how innocently naive Alfie was for thinking they would all have a lovely holiday in the countryside.

But still, she was looking forward to that summer move. The complete change of scenery would be a wonderful experience in itself. And with some luck, she might even find that delightful brook to dip her toes in.

Chapter Twelve

Stella desperately wanted to stretch her aching limbs and her sore back. But there was no space for her to do much more than twitch her nose inside the rattling old carriage that was taking them to the Bosworths' summer residence in Buckinghamshire. Already, Mrs Burch had admonished her twice for fidgeting. So rather than risk any further anger from the housekeeper, Stella decided to keep still and endure the discomfort.

And in a way, she was lucky, she supposed. Because even though she had been crammed into the carriage along with the other young maids, as well as Cook and Mrs Burch, at least she was sitting by an open window. Next to her, Cook's ample body took up a sizeable portion of the hard wooden seat. Packed together like sardines, Stella could feel the woman's sweaty heat. But the breeze coming in through the window made the experience just about bearable.

The view outside made up for a lot of the unpleasantness of the long journey too. They had left London some time ago and were now travelling through lusciously green countryside. Perhaps when they reached the next village, the coachman would want to rest the horses again, she hoped. Which meant they could escape the stifling confines of the carriage for a short while.

Lily and Margaret were chatting excitedly, happy to get out of London for the summer. Stella had been looking forward to that as well, but right now, she didn't share the maids' enthusiasm.

If this is what travelling is like, she groaned inwardly, *then I think I might prefer to simply stay in the city.*

Their carriage had set off at the crack of dawn, ahead of the others, and she had been told they would arrive at the country estate late in the afternoon or early in the evening, depending on how well the horses kept up.

Again, she smirked, *the wellbeing of the horses is more important than ours.*

But there was an upside to this arrangement as well, she reminded herself. The Bosworth family wouldn't be leaving until the next morning. So that meant a full day without the constant supervision and criticism of Mrs Bosworth. A comforting thought that made her smile.

Especially since their mistress had done more than double her usual amount of supervising and bitter complaining the day before, when they had needed to pack for the journey.

All day long, and under the watchful eye of Mrs Bosworth, the maids had been frantically busy filling travel cases with everything the mistress deemed necessary for their summer stay at the country estate. Clothes made up the biggest part of those necessities, evidently.

Making herself even more insufferable than normal, the mistress had pointed out which item of clothing needed to go where.

"And be careful," she warned them nearly every time. "If I find so much as a crease or a little tear in anything, I will personally see to it that you mend it. And any damage is coming out of your wages."

All the maids were anxious and on edge, which only slowed them down and made the day seem even longer and harder than it already was.

Stella in particular seemed to have fallen from favour. She would have sworn their mistress had it in for her.

"Emma," Mrs Bosworth shouted when they were packing the final two cases. But Stella hadn't reacted at first, since Mrs Bosworth was in the habit of randomly calling her maids Emma.

And that name had been hissed and yelled quite a lot that day.

It was only when Mrs Bosworth roughly grabbed her by the arm that Stella realised it had been her the mistress was sniping at.

"Are you deaf?" Mrs Bosworth asked, fixating the girl with her cold blue-grey eyes.

"No, ma'am."

"Then why don't you answer when you're spoken to? I trust basic manners aren't too much to ask, even from a simple maid like you."

"I'm sorry, Mrs Bosworth. I didn't know you meant me."

"Who else would I be talking to, you stupid girl?"

Oh, I don't know, Stella thought sarcastically. *Just about anyone else who you call Emma, my dear Mrs Meanworth*.

"You've placed that dress in the wrong case," Mrs Bosworth carped. She shook Stella's arm violently, and pointed at one of the other cases. "I told you to put it in that one."

Stella bit her lip. She distinctly remembered Mrs Bosworth saying it had to go in the one where she had carefully placed it. But she knew better than to point that out. Telling Mrs Bosworth she was wrong would only make her angrier.

Letting go of Stella's arm, Mrs Bosworth grabbed the offending dress and threw it at her.

"Now do as you're told," she barked. "And make sure you fold that dress properly. It's a disgrace the way you shoved it into that case. Do you wish me to look like some disheveled peasant woman this summer perhaps?"

"No, ma'am," Stella replied meekly.

She was sure even the most common countryside milk maid would look like a nicer, kinder person than Mrs Meanworth in her prettiest dress.

When everything had finally been packed, the footmen were instructed to carry the heavy cases to the stables, where the coachmen would load them onto the carriages. The maids were told to carry the smaller boxes – many of which contained Mrs Bosworth's extensive collection of hats.

"You'd think the missus is going to change her clothes at least three times a day," Lily had muttered under her breath while they were hurrying between the house and the stables.

"I swear she's taking enough hats to supply the whole of Buckinghamshire," Margaret said.

"Just be glad she's not making us move the silverware as well," Pete joked when he took the boxes the maids were carrying.

"Please don't give her any ideas," Stella begged.

He treated her to one of his warm, friendly smiles.

"Are you all right?" he asked. "You look distraught."

Stella nodded.

"Her ladyship was in her element again, I'm afraid. But she didn't hit me this time, so I guess that's something."

"Someone ought to hit *her* for a change if you ask me," Pete scoffed.

"Don't talk nonsense," Stella cautioned him, fearful Mrs Bosworth might show up behind their backs at any moment. "What good would that do to anyone?"

"Not much probably," Pete said. "But I would love to see the look on that arrogant face of hers right after I've smacked it."

He held up the palm of his hand, conjuring up the scene in his mind. "I think I would sleep very well that night," he grinned.

"Not without a roof over your head you wouldn't," she tempered. "Which is why we keep our hands to ourselves and our mouths shut. What would your father do without you?"

"Relax," he answered. "Nothing wrong with a little daydreaming. Doesn't mean I want to do it. I'm not stupid."

Rattling along in the old carriage on their way to the estate, Stella smiled at the memory.

She admired Pete for his strength of character as much as for his ability to make her laugh.

She wished he were travelling in the coach with her, because she felt she could do with some liberating laughter right now. But Pete would be arriving a day later. His father was the head coachman, so they would be driving the family carriage.

When Stella looked out the window, all she could see was vast green countryside and a blue sky. It was even more beautiful than she had imagined. This was the sort of place where poets came to write their poetry, she was sure of it. Only having lived in London all her life, she wasn't used to so much open space. Here, there were no ugly factory chimneys spewing their dirty smoke up into the air. Only fields and meadows as far as the eye could see.

She wished she could hop out of the carriage and skip barefoot through the grass. Sadly though, all she could do was lean back against the hard bench and watch the landscape as it slowly slid past the window.

By the time they arrived at the estate, dusk was slowly setting in. But there was still enough daylight for Stella to get a sense of the scale and the splendour of the Bosworth estate. Ivy covered large swaths of the sand-coloured brick walls. There was a large garden around the mansion, with neatly trimmed lawns and bushes. Stella spotted a water-spraying fountain as well, encircled by stone lions and ornaments.

The Bosworths' London residence was a grand abode, but it was nothing compared to their country estate. To Stella's eyes, this place looked suitable for a king, even though she knew perfectly well that the Bosworths didn't have any noble titles at all. Pete had told her how Mr Bosworth's grandfather had accumulated most of his wealth through breeding and selling horses, which was why the family still owned a stud farm and livery in the countryside.

A handful of footmen were waiting for them when the carriage came to a halt. Mrs Burch immediately took charge, seemingly fit and fresh, as if they hadn't just spent the entire day cooped up in that uncomfortable carriage. Perhaps the housekeeper was just as happy to be in the countryside as the others, Stella pondered.

Under Mrs Burch's instructions, everyone began to unload the carriages. The footmen groaned when they took hold of one of Alfie's cases.

Probably stuffed with books, Stella smiled to herself.

Casting one more look at the beautiful surroundings and another at the huge country mansion, she wasn't too sure she would have much time for reading or relaxation.

But she would worry about that tomorrow.

First, she wanted to get to bed as soon as possible. Because tomorrow evening, the Bosworth family would be arriving.

And Pete.

Chapter Thirteen

Ever since her parents had passed away, Stella hadn't known a summer as cheerful and happy as the one she spent at the Bosworth country estate. Every day when she woke up, she quickly ventured outside for a few precious minutes. She enjoyed filling her lungs with the fresh morning breeze. And with her eyes closed, she would inhale the scent of wildflowers, while she tried to imagine what they looked like.

It was far from a holiday for a simple maid like her of course, but she still managed to find joy in the little things. In birdsong, sunsets, buzzing insects and playful squirrels. And waking up with the first rays of sunshine touching her face felt infinitely better than awakening to the tune of the shrill voices of Mrs Burch or Mrs Bosworth.

She even succeeded in finding a brook, just like the one in her daydreams. It was perfectly peaceful, and in one particular spot, the brook had a secluded bank that eased slowly into the water – making it ideal to wade into and cool her tired feet. Her duties at the house usually kept her too busy to go there often unfortunately. But whenever she got a chance to escape, the brook was one of her favourite places.

That, and the stables obviously, where she knew she was likely to find Pete. With him, she could talk about everything. And he often seemed like the only person capable of understanding her. While she had a soft spot for Alfie, she was painfully aware of the huge divide that separated them.

With Pete however, it was different.

They ate at the same table, and their lives were plagued by similar problems. She could tell him about her maid's life, he could tell her about his life at the stables, and they would comprehend and appreciate each other. The world of a rich child – even a kind one like Alfie – was simply too far removed from their own.

Still, the three of them enjoyed whatever precious little time they spent together. Pete even taught Stella and Alfie to play cards that summer. It was a guilty pleasure that Alfie in particular liked to revel in. If his mother found out her darling son was engaging in an activity as common and as crass as card playing, there would be no end to her fury and outrage. Which made their secret games all the more exciting to him.

And as their summer stay drew to a close, he seemed determined to squeeze every ounce of joy out of their meetings. He lost most of the games, but that didn't seem to bother him in the slightest.

So that evening, when he threw down his losing hand, the long sigh he let out wasn't because of his bad fortune.

"That's it for me, I'm afraid," he said, the melancholy painfully plain in his voice.

"One more?" Stella suggested. "Maybe your luck will turn this time."

"No, I need to get back to the house. Before Mother notices I'm missing."

Pete gathered up the cards and shuffled them.

"Thank you, dear friends," Alfie said.

"For what?" Pete asked with a smile, while he put away the cards. "For beating you at cards most every time?"

Alfie laughed. "No, for making this summer the best one I've ever had."

"That goes for me too," Stella said. "I haven't had this much fun in years. So thank you both."

"You're welcome," Pete replied as he stood up.

Alfie followed his example and dusted down his clothes. Wouldn't want Mother to know he had been at the stables again.

"Well, I had best be off then," he said, reluctant to leave. "We will soon be heading back to London, and I don't know if we will get another chance to meet up before we go."

He took a few hesitant steps towards the stable doors, and then stopped. Stella thought she saw him drawing in breath and straightening his shoulders. To bolster his courage perhaps?

"Good night, Alfie," she said, basking in the pleasant afterglow of the moment while simultaneously feeling sorry for the boy.

"Good night, Stella. Good night, Pete. See you back home soon."

Stella smiled at him and Pete merely nodded, probably uneasy about all these conflicting emotions, she assumed.

"So sad," she said once Alfie had left.

"What is?" Pete asked. He seemed to be fidgeting, unsure about what to do next.

"To see poor Alfie like that. It's clear he's so much happier out here. More at ease as well. But still his mother's shadow looms over him. As if she's some sort of spectre that possesses him."

Pete shrugged. "The lad has it in him to become a fine gentleman one day. But that won't happen if he continues to be a scared little rabbit scurrying in fright over his Mama's every single word."

"Don't be so harsh on him, Pete."

"It's true though. He may be young, but if he doesn't start standing up to Mrs Meanworth a bit more, he'll end up being just as spineless as his feeble father."

He smiled bitterly and shook his head. "Which is probably exactly what the Ice Queen wants anyway."

"What do you mean? Surely, she wants her son to grow into a strong man who forges his path to success. Isn't that every mother's dream?"

Pete snorted derisively. "Does she strike you as a normal woman then?"

"Not really," Stella had to admit.

"No, if you ask me, she's trying to make him the same sort of laughable weakling as his father."

"But what could she possibly gain from having a son like that?"

Pete looked at her intensely. "The same thing she gains from her husband. Money and control."

As much as she hated the thought, Stella had to accept his point. Mrs Bosworth certainly struck her as the kind of woman who wanted to control the people around her. Would Alfie be strong enough to break that spell?

She wasn't too sure unfortunately.

"I've got something for you," Pete said, interrupting her dark thoughts.

"For me?" she answered in surprise.

"A small present. Nothing fancy."

She couldn't remember when she had last received a gift.

"Close your eyes and hold out your hand," he told her.

She did as he asked, and waited, not knowing what to expect. She heard him rummaging about somewhere, and then he gently pressed something into her palm. It felt cold and fairly heavy. Opening her eyes again, she saw it was a horseshoe.

"It's from Atlantis," Pete explained. "He's an amazing horse and, well, they say horseshoes bring good luck. Since I figured you could use some..."

Suddenly, he seemed to be feeling awkward.

"Also, I thought our time here together was so wonderful, it ought to be remembered by something."

His brown eyes studied her reaction. "You don't have to take it if you don't want to."

"I love it," she said. "That's so thoughtful of you." She gave him a broad smile.

"I'm glad you like it," he said, visibly relieved.

"But I haven't got anything to give you."

"No need," he smiled.

They stood there for a while, gazing at each other happily, and suddenly, without thinking about it, she wrapped her arms around him. He hesitated at first, but then he gave in to the embrace. For a short while, they stood there, in each other's arms, feeling the warmth of each other's breaths on their shoulders.

Then, Stella had to pull away. As she looked into his eyes again, they seemed longing, as if something had been taken from him. Stella felt the same. But she slowly shook her head.

"It's too dangerous," she said, not sure herself what exactly she meant by that.

"I know," Pete said. "But it feels good. It feels less lonely."

Stella knew exactly what he meant by that. For a moment the world had felt like it stopped spinning – like all that mattered was contained within that one embrace.

"I'd better go, Pete," she said.

Although he tried to hide it, he looked disappointed.

In passing, she pressed a quick kiss on his cheek. And even though she didn't turn around to see his reaction, she pictured a happy grin slowly taking over his beautiful face.

Chapter Fourteen

Outside, the city was firmly in the grips of a wet and chilly autumn. Down in the kitchen however, the heat emanating from the wood fire in the oven kept the staff warm, while they chatted excitedly over breakfast. But even without the roaring oven, Stella doubted if anyone would have noticed the cold this morning. Because the only thing on every staff member's mind seemed to be the juicy piece of gossip Pete had shared.

Mr Bosworth was going on an expedition to Africa!

The news was greeted with astonished gasps and animated chatter around the servants' table.

"To Africa?" the eldest maid Lily asked. "For how long?"

Pete shrugged. "Couple of months maybe? Half a year? Who knows? I only briefly overheard him talking to his wife about his plans when I took his horse. I couldn't exactly hang around and listen."

"Who in his right mind would want to go to Africa? It's devilishly hot there," Tommy said. "Give me English weather any time."

"That's not what you said when it was raining so hard last week," Pete joked, poking his friend in the ribs.

"But why?" Lily wondered. "Why would a boring, grey mouse like Mr Bosworth want to go to Africa?"

"To get far away from his wife?" Pete replied, to a big round of laughter.

"Butterflies," Stella said.

"Eh?" Tommy asked, revealing his missing teeth.

"Mr Bosworth collects butterflies," she explained, remembering her first visit to his study. "I should imagine they have lots of exotic butterflies in Africa."

The man's fascination was nothing short of an obsession. She wouldn't have been surprised if he dreamt of butterflies at night.

"Cor," Lily exclaimed. "Imagine going to another world just to chase after a bunch of fluttering insects!"

"It's not right being that wealthy," Tommy said. "Travelling to some dreadfully hot and faraway place, simply because you don't have anything better to do with your money."

"I hope he gets eaten by a lion," Lily sniggered with a mean smile.

"That's cruel," Pete objected. "All that fat would be sure to give the poor lion indigestion."

Everybody laughed – even more so when Tommy pressed his mouth to his forearm and made disgusting fart noises.

"Do you think the mistress will be nicer when her husband is away?" young Esther asked timidly.

"I'm afraid not, dear," Stella said. "She barely takes notice of him when he's around. So I don't think his going abroad will make much of a difference."

The scullery maid was visibly disappointed. Who could blame her, she was only eleven. So Stella tried to cheer the girl up.

"But I suppose there is some good news for you," she said with a smile.

"How's that?"

"With Mr Bosworth gone, there will be one set of dishes less for you to clean."

"The master does eat a lot," Esther chuckled.

Stella gave her a wink. "Told you there was a bright side."

"I hate to spoil it for you, ladies," Pete said. "But with her husband out of the way, I'm willing to bet good money we'll be seeing even more of Mrs Bosworth's music teacher."

He spoke those last two words with so much sarcasm, it made several people round the table grin. Everyone knew what really went on between Charles Preston and Mrs Bosworth.

And there was nothing musical about it.

Pete's prophetic words rang in Stella's ears hours later, when she was tasked with serving tea during Mr Preston's visit to his so-called music pupil.

Their mistress made a spectacle of herself, Stella felt, by cooing and fawning over him the way she did.

"Oh, Charles," Mrs Bosworth sighed longingly. "Will you keep me company while that wretched husband of mine is off chasing butterflies?"

"I could certainly increase the frequency of my visits," he replied rather coolly. "If that's what you want."

"Of course it's what I want!"

Stella thought Mrs Bosworth almost sounded insulted by her lover's lack of enthusiasm. The lady of the house grabbed her guest by the arm, beseechingly.

"Why are you being so distant, Charles? It's bad enough my husband loves his bugs more than he loves his own wife. So don't you start giving me the cold shoulder as well, you hear? It's cruel, and I shan't tolerate it."

Stella couldn't believe her ears. Was Mrs Bosworth complaining about her husband not loving her, when she herself never spoke a friendly word to him? All the woman ever gave him was spiteful scorn and vitriol.

Charles Preston merely laughed. "Seriously, Josephine? Love? Is that what you're after in your darling husband? I think you mean attention, dear. Isn't that what you really want? From any man? Attention?"

Mrs Bosworth pouted her lips and turned her face away from him, like a petulant little girl.

"Love, attention – what does it matter? It's all the same thing."

As distasteful as their affair was in Stella's opinion, she was equally intrigued by the way these two talked to each other. With them, it was always more like a sparring match than a conversation. Mrs Bosworth clearly had strong feelings about Mr Preston, but he seemed to enjoy keeping her at arm's length. And of course, his playing hard to get only served to stoke up Mrs Bosworth's passions further.

Could it be that the mistress had finally found her match with this man? An ice prince for the ice queen?

"Don't turn your pretty little nose up in anger like that, my dear," he soothed. Taking her chin with his strong hand, he made her face him again. "You know I prefer to look at your beautiful eyes instead of the luscious curls on the back of your head."

"Do you now?" Mrs Bosworth grinned. Edging a little closer to him on the sofa, she whispered, "Anything else you prefer looking at?"

"Hmm, let me think about that one for a while," he teased.

"You scoundrel," she said, playfully slapping him on the chest with the back of her hand.

Discreetly, Stella shook her head. Charles Preston was a mystery to her. This man was so hard to read. One minute he was playing it cool. Then in a heartbeat, he changed tack and spoke smooth words of sweetness.

There was something about him that made Stella distrust him. Maybe because whenever he laughed, he could switch back to a straight face within a matter of seconds. Or maybe it was the way he smiled, while his voice sounded completely neutral.

"Emma," Mrs Bosworth barked suddenly, startling Stella.

"Yes, Mrs Bosworth?"

"Why are you still here?"

"Because I thought you always wanted me to keep the teacups full, ma'am."

"Well, they're full now and we won't be needing you further. Dismissed."

"Yes, ma'am," Stella curtsied. *With pleasure*, she added silently.

Glad to leave the two lovers to their own devices, she closed the door behind her and shivered. Not in a million years would she want to trade places with her mistress. Mrs Bosworth had all the material comforts anyone could wish for, but other than that, her existence was as empty as her cold heart.

While she made her way to the kitchen, she wondered if Mrs Bosworth had always been like this. Or if maybe once upon a time, long ago, this mean, vicious woman had been happy. Stella imagined her mistress must have been young and beautiful once, with dreams of her own? What had happened to those dreams? What had happened to that young woman?

Arriving in the busy kitchen, Stella decided it wasn't her problem. All she knew was that she didn't like the present Mrs Bosworth. And everyone in the household would agree with her on that one.

Whatever unhappiness or misery Alfie's mother experienced was ultimately of her own doing, Stella concluded.

Chapter Fifteen

"My condolences, Josephine," Mrs Bosworth's older sister said while stirring a spoonful of sugar through her tea. "I came over as soon as I heard the tragic news."

"Thank you, Anna," Mrs Bosworth replied. "I'm so glad you are here with me at this sad time."

"That's what sisters are for," her sibling nodded with grave sympathy. "How did it happen?"

Standing in the background, Stella thought the tone of that last question was distinctly different. It sounded more like Mrs Bosworth's sister was fishing for gory details or juicy gossip. These rich people were odd like that.

"Some kind of fever, the letter said." Mrs Bosworth dabbed delicately at the corner of her eye with a handkerchief, even though Stella had yet to see her mistress shed any tears over the sudden death of her husband.

Even when wearing nothing but black, the lady of the house still managed to look elegant and handsome. Stella was fairly sure mourning attire was supposed to be modest and subdued, out of respect for the dead. But of course, that simply wasn't Mrs Bosworth's style. Instead, she had instructed her dressmaker to create something more in line with her vain and egocentric personality.

Earlier that morning, Stella had had to spend nearly half an hour helping to arrange Mrs Bosworth's black veil just right.

But the result had the desired effect: to anyone unfamiliar with the lady's mean character, Mrs Bosworth looked stunning.

"Fever," her sister repeated. "And right at the end of his expedition too. But that's Africa for you, I suppose. What on earth possessed Reginald to go to a dreadful corner of the world like that?"

"Butterflies of course, Anna darling."

"Of course," her sister tutted, rolling her eyes.

Stella couldn't believe these two women were talking about Mr Bosworth so condescendingly and disapprovingly mere days after that fateful letter had arrived. He might have been a seemingly pathetic figure, but surely the dead deserved a little bit more respect than this?

"How sad," Anna said.

"Quite," Mrs Bosworth replied drily.

You don't sound very sad though, Stella thought. Mrs Bosworth kept a tight lock on her heart and her true feelings. And very few people – if any – possessed the key.

"What will you do now?" Mrs Bosworth's sister enquired before taking another sip of tea.

"Emma," Mrs Bosworth said suddenly. "My sister's teacup is only a quarter full. Refill it, you idle child."

Stella obliged immediately, while the ladies ignored her as if she were invisible.

"What shall I do?" Mrs Bosworth repeated her sister's question. "Same as always, naturally. Fend for myself and carry on."

"I admire your courage and your will, Josephine. You're so strong."

"A woman has to be, dear, if she is to survive in this cruel and unjust world."

Her sister nodded.

"And how is the boy?"

Mrs Bosworth sighed. "I'm not sure. Ever since I informed him, Alfred has locked himself away in his room. He doesn't even open the door for food."

That was true. Stella had been sent up several times to bring Alfie his meals. But when she knocked on his door, he didn't answer.

"Alfie, it's me," she would whisper.

His reply, uttered in a weak and quiet voice, was always the same. "Just leave the tray by the door, Stella."

"Okay. But please let me know if you need anything else."

All she ever got from him however was silence. So she was very worried about him. More worried probably than his own mother.

"Give him some time," Mrs Bosworth's sister said encouragingly. "It must be hard for the boy. He hasn't got your tremendous strength of character yet."

"I am all he has now," Mrs Bosworth replied. "I have to be strong for him. And I shall have to redouble my parental duties and guidance. Not that he ever got much of that from his father, mind you."

"He is fortunate to have you as his mother."

Mrs Bosworth nodded at the compliment.

"But then of course," her sister continued, "the boy will be off to boarding school soon. Which shall do both of you good, I suppose. It will bring you more freedom and time to yourself, and provide him with some welcome distraction."

Mrs Bosworth shifted in her seat.

"I have been thinking about that, Anna. And I'm not sure I am ready yet to let him go. He is the joy of my life. Without him, I fear the house will be terribly empty."

That almost sounded like a heartfelt emotion to Stella's ears. She even thought she detected a faint hint of potential tears in Mrs Bosworth's voice.

So the lady of the house had feelings after all!

Unless she was faking it, pretending to be the grieving widow and mourning mother, for her sister's benefit.

A strange mixture of sympathy, contempt and fascination swirled inside Stella's mind. The more she learned about Josephine Bosworth, the less sure she grew what to think of her. Could it truly be that Alfred held a special place in this woman's ice-cold heart? Would she be capable of that sort of maternal affection?

Mrs Bosworth's sister cleared her throat. "But what about financial matters? Without meaning to intrude into such private affairs obviously."

"Obviously," Mrs Bosworth replied with a fine smile.

Her sister did her best to appear calm and nonchalant, but Mrs Bosworth intentionally drew out the suspense a bit more by taking a sip of tea before answering.

"Reginald's will states that I should be Alfred's guardian until his twenty-first birthday. After which he inherits everything."

"Everything?" her sister asked. Stella thought the woman's tone was a bizarre combination of shocked surprise about the significance of that arrangement... and malicious delight at her younger sibling's misfortune.

"With some basic provisions for me of course," Mrs Bosworth said, trying to hide her displeasure. "But other than that, Alfred gets everything the day he turns twenty-one. The house, the countryside estate, and all of the family's assets."

"He will be a very wealthy young man then," her sister stated.

"Quite," Mrs Bosworth agreed.

The room was awkwardly silent, as both women decided to sip some more tea.

As soon as the social visit was over, Stella rushed back to the kitchen. She simply had to tell Pete about everything she had heard. Alfie would be in for a difficult time, with his mother clearly envying him for his inheritance while also being appointed as his guardian. She hoped Pete would know how they could help or even protect their friend.

But the stable boy wasn't to be found in the kitchen when she got there. Several other members of the staff were however.

"Well?" they asked her eagerly. "Did you find out any more news?"

Word of the master's death had travelled fast through the servants' quarters. Fanciful gossip mingled with facts, and Stella was hesitant to add to the rumour mill. But she knew she had to give them something, if she was to have any hope of not creating even more animosity towards herself.

"Mr Bosworth has left his entire fortune to his son," she said.

"Cor," Lily answered with vicious glee. "Nothing for the missus then?"

"Not much, from what I've heard," Stella shrugged. "But she will be managing the boy and all his wealth until his twenty-first birthday."

"Plenty of time then for her to turn the boy into the same kind of docile weakling as her late husband," Cook said.

"That's good news for you, Cook," Lily sniggered. "Because she can bait him with food. The little runt's already well on his way of becoming a porky pig like his father. Oink oink."

Lily and Margaret hooted with laughter, while they made pig noises. Stella wanted to smack them in the face for their rude mockery. But she couldn't do that, for obvious reasons. If the maids knew the real extent of her secret friendship with Alfie, there would be no end to their ridicule. Worse yet, they might decide to use the information against her.

She needed to talk to Pete. Sooner rather than later. Because he was the only one she could fully trust. In any matter.

Chapter Sixteen

It took a while for Alfie to come out of his room after his father's death. But as soon as he did, he secretly arranged to meet with Stella and Pete at the stables.

Hidden away in Atlantis' box, the three of them sat on a fresh pile of clean straw bedding, with Alfie in the middle. The boy's favourite horse curiously sniffed at his young master, and then gave him a friendly nudge with his soft nose before resuming to chomp down on some hay.

"See," Stella smiled. "Even Atlantis is here to comfort you."

Alfie merely nodded and stared in the direction of his horse, although Stella had the impression he was gazing past the animal, into some invisible distance.

"I don't know what to feel," he said. His eyes were still red from crying, but at the moment he seemed calm. "I'm supposed to be sad, aren't I?"

"You're not supposed to be or feel anything," Pete said. "Either you feel things, or you don't. No use beating yourself up over it."

"And maybe you are feeling lots of things," Stella added. "But you're simply too overwhelmed to realise what's going through your mind."

"It's just–" Alfie began. "I feel like the man who died was a stranger. I mean, he was my father, and I know Mother must be devastated. But me? I don't feel an awful lot."

Stella wasn't convinced about his mother being devastated. But she wasn't going to tell the boy that obviously.

He looked at her and Pete with sorrowful eyes begging for answers to explain the mess of emotions he was experiencing.

"Does that make me a bad son?" he asked miserably. "Shouldn't a son be mourning his dead father?"

"Of course you're not a bad son, Alfie," she answered immediately. "If my father had barely ever spoken to me, I suppose I wouldn't have been sad either when he died."

Placing a hand on his shoulder, she added, "It's not your fault your father was more interested in his insects than you."

She realised that had sounded more harsh than she intended, so she was quick to apologise. "I'm sorry, I didn't mean to presume."

"No, you're right," he replied. "We were never close. But this whole situation still makes me feel strange."

Pete scratched his chin. "Strange in what way?"

Alfie took a moment to reflect on his feelings.

"I'm afraid," he said. "Yes, that's it. I'm not sad, but afraid rather."

"Afraid?" Stella asked. "What for?"

"The future. I've seen my father's will. It says Mother is to be my legal guardian until I'm twenty-one." He wrapped his arms around his knees. "But that day is still so far off. What will she do in the meantime? She can do anything she wants."

Slowly, tears started filling his eyes again.

"What if she decides to sell the horses? Or my books? Who's to stop her? Or," he stammered, "what if she wants to send you all away?"

"Hey, stop worrying like that," Stella replied, and gave him a hug. "It will all be all right. Your mother won't suddenly turn into a monster just because your father is no longer among us."

Pete chuckled. "At least not more of a monster than she already is."

Stella shot him a reprimanding glare. Now wasn't the time for his clever remarks. Even though he was right, they didn't need to remind Alfie how horrible his mother was. Not when the boy was contemplating what she might come up with to make his life even more unpleasant.

"Suppose she marries Mr Preston?" Alfie said.

That was a distinct possibility, Stella had to concede. And looking over at Pete, she could tell from his face that he was thinking the same thing.

"Why would she want to marry her music teacher?" she asked instead, feigning innocent ignorance in a vain attempt to dismiss the notion.

Alfie threw her a look that told her he didn't believe the whole music teacher ruse any more than anyone else in the household.

"You shouldn't fret over such things," she urged him. "Whatever she decides to do, your mother will have to remain in mourning first. So you just concentrate on yourself in the meantime."

"Besides," Pete blurted out, trying to help in steering the conversation onto safer grounds. "Your mother can't keep you here forever. Don't forget you'll be off to boarding school soon."

Stella felt it wiser not to share what she had overheard Mrs Bosworth telling her sister on the subject of boarding school. Surely, the woman didn't seriously intend to keep her son that close to her at all times?

Looking at it from that perspective, she almost wished Alfie would leave very soon indeed. For his sake.

Even though the idea of his departure stung her a little. She knew she would miss him once he was gone.

"Ah yes," Alfie said flatly. "Boarding school."

So he didn't seem too eager about leaving home either, Stella thought.

"You're not excited about going to boarding school?" Pete exclaimed, as if he simply couldn't understand why you wouldn't be looking forward to the prospect.

Alfie shook his head and stared at his feet.

"Why not?" Pete asked.

"Don't know. It's just so... different."

"That's the whole idea," Pete laughed. "Cheer up, Alfie. You'll meet plenty of lads your age, and you'll finally be away from here."

"I know, but it's still scary. I've never had any friends besides you two. What if they don't like me?"

"Come on, Alfie," Stella said. "What's not to like? You're smart. You're kind."

"Handsome little bugger too," Pete quipped, giving him a playful little shove of the elbow that made Alfie giggle slightly.

"You'll find friends in no time," Stella promised, hoping that was true. "And think of all the books you can read!"

"Exactly," Pete said. "Don't you know what the likes of Stella and me would give to learn the things you'll be able to study? Every time you're back for the holidays, you can tell us all about the clever things they taught you."

Alfie's mood lightened up a little more. "I guess you're right."

"There you go then," Stella said contentedly.

"I'll miss you both dearly though," he said. "I'd write you letters, but I don't think Mother would like it very much if I wrote to the maid and the stable boy."

"We know you won't forget about us," Pete assured him. "Besides, we're always busy here anyway. Chances are we wouldn't have time to read your letters."

"But tell you what," Stella suggested. "If you promise to think of us every day, in the evening let's say, then we'll do the same. That way, we'll all be thinking of each other at the same time."

Alfie's eyes lit up. "Our shoulders won't be touching like they are now," he said excitedly. "But our minds will! I think it's a great idea, Stella."

"I'm glad you like it," she replied. "And I'm happy to see that you seem a bit less sad."

He got up and brushed the straw from his clothes. "I feel so much better. Thanks to you two."

"At your service, Master Bosworth," Pete joked while performing a deep bow, complete with a flourish of the hand.

Alfie giggled and said his goodbyes.

When he had left, Stella sank into her own unhappy thoughts. Alfie had the chance to get away from this place. And from his domineering mother. He would pack his bags and go to boarding school.

And later, once he was a man, he could venture out into the world, to do whatever he pleased, go wherever he wanted, and become whomever he desired to be.

Stella envied him for that. Because she had no such outlook on life. She was doomed to be nothing but a maid. If not for Mrs Bosworth, then in some other household with cold and distant masters. One day, if she got lucky, she would meet a man with whom she would raise a brood of children and grandchildren.

Until she was old and grey. The end.

Oh, what she wouldn't give to escape that sorry fate! And to escape from Mrs Bosworth in the first place. But right now, she saw no way out. All she could do was keep her head down and do her work every day, while saving up whatever she could from her pitiful wages.

As long as she had Pete to talk to however, it wouldn't be too bad. And maybe her mind was blowing this situation out of proportion. Mrs Bosworth might have been mean and cold-hearted, but she wouldn't be scheming to do anything truly evil, would she?

After all, Stella told herself, despite appearances, the woman was hardly the devil incarnate.

Chapter Seventeen

Underneath her warm and cozy bed sheets, Josephine woke up from a deeply gratifying slumber. Slowly, to prolong the lazy joy of the moment, she stretched her arms and legs. Then, with her eyes still closed and sporting a blissful smile on her face, she rolled over towards the other side of the bed. But when she reached out with her arm, to her surprise, she found nothing there.

"Charles?" she softly called out into the room, her voice low and thick.

"My love?" His smiling voice came from a corner of the room.

Raising herself up on her elbows, she blinked against the rays of sunshine coming through the curtains. "Oh, there you are," she said when she spotted him sitting in a chair.

"I am indeed," he grinned. A shining example of masculine virility, he looked perfectly at ease and confident, leaning against the back of the chair and with his legs stretched out before him.

"What are you doing over there?" she yawned.

"Admiring you, my sleeping beauty."

"Sleeping beauty?" she smiled. "Does that make you my Prince Charming?"

"If you so desire."

"I do." Nimble and graceful as a cat, she brought herself to sit upright in bed. "Come over here and kiss me, good prince. To break the awful spell."

He chuckled. "And what spell would that be?"

"Why, the dreadful curse of mourning obviously."

She let herself fall back into bed and sighed. "Can you believe I'm supposed to grieve for that ridiculous swine for two years? Two whole years! Who came up with that idea?"

"Etiquette, dear," he replied as he stood up and walked over to the bed. "The unwritten rules that govern our society." He smiled at her and gave her a kiss.

"Well, then those unwritten rules are stupid," she pouted daintily.

"It's only two years," he said. "And after that..." –he teasingly caressed a loose lock of her hair– "you will be free to do whatever you want, with whomever you please."

Suddenly, she jumped out of bed and went over to the mirror. "Unfortunately, a few years after that, I shan't have enough money to support myself half-decently. Because my darling son will inherit his father's entire fortune."

Running her fingers through her long curly hair, she sulked, "I look a complete mess."

"No, you don't," he said, giving her a little kiss on her bare shoulder. "You look just fine the way you are."

She huffed in disbelief at his remark. "You men have it easy," she complained while she started brushing her hair angrily. "All you need to do is throw on some clothes, run some wax through your hair, and you're done."

"What can I say?" he laughed. "I guess we men simply possess charm and beauty by nature."

Having finished with her hair, she put down her brush and sighed deeply. "Oh Charles, what am I to do?"

"About what? Is this a wardrobe question?"

"No, about this affair with the inheritance, I mean. As soon as the boy comes of age, he gets everything and I'll be left destitute."

"Destitute," he chuckled. "Come now, Josephine. The will granted you an allowance."

"An allowance? A degrading pittance, you mean. Certainly not the generous means that would allow me to continue living to the high standards I am used to. I shall be forced to beg my son for money every month."

She reached for her corset, slipped it on, and waited for him to help her tighten it.

"Alfie is a good boy," he said while lacing her up. "I am certain he would give you all the money your little heart desired."

"Perhaps. But that would give him control over me! And I could never allow that to happen. No man shall have control over me. Not even my own son."

"But what if..." –with a sudden sharp tug he pulled the strings of her corset tight, briefly cutting off her breath– "What if he let you manage all his money? Then *you* would control *him.*"

"Why would he let me do that?"

"His father let you run most of his affairs, didn't he?"

"His father was a spineless weakling."

"Then you simply turn the son into the same sort of spineless weakling as the father."

Intrigued by his sinister idea, she stared at his reflection in the mirror. "How?"

He laughed. "Surely, I don't need to tell you how to break a man's will? To crush his spirit? And make him your obedient slave?"

Charles let his hand glide softly over her shoulders, bringing goosebumps to her skin and sending shivers down her spine.

"You still have several years until the boy turns twenty-one," he continued. "That should be plenty of time for you to mould him into the exact shape and form you want him to be."

Turning around, she studied his face. His dark eyes were almost glowing with determination, and his moustache curled mischievously around his smiling lips.

Something about the intensity that was apparent in her lover's features frightened her. Yet at the same time, it made him all the more irresistible, and pulled her closer to him.

"I can do that," she nodded slowly. "It wouldn't be the first time I made a man bend to my wishes."

"Precisely," he said with a twinkle in his eyes. Then he licked his lips. "I'm afraid there is no other way, Josephine. As sad as the poor boy's fate might seem to some."

"Poor boy?!" Josephine spat. "What about poor me? It's never about me and my troubles, is it?" Her angry face reddened. "But who was the one who gave birth to him in a torment of pain, I ask you? Whose body bears the marks but mine?"

Raising his hands to ward off her sudden outburst, he said, "I know, my love." He stepped closer to her and tenderly took her by the shoulders. "But now you have the chance to make it all worth it. Your years of suffering under a man's rule are over. Now that Reginald is dead, you will have all the power."

Calming down, she nodded. He was right. It was her turn to firmly hold the reins.

"So," he asked. "What are you going to do?"

She cleared her throat and stood a little taller.

"First of all, Alfie won't be attending any boarding school. Heaven knows what they would teach him there. Nothing but a stuffy collection of boring old men instructing the next generation how to rule the world and oppress women."

"Not the kind of influence you want," he agreed with a grin.

Enthused by her own train of thought, she sat down in front of the mirror again and let her mind race over the possibilities.

"I need to keep Alfie at home with me, under my constant supervision. His tutors can continue to educate him privately." She laughed. "That will probably work out cheaper as well than to send him away to an expensive boarding school."

"I like your thinking," he grinned. "More money for you. And remember, you need to restrict the boy drastically. Get him to ask permission for absolutely everything he does. More classes, less riding. Until being dependent on you becomes the most natural thing for him."

"Leave it to me," she said. "I know what I am doing." She buttoned up her blouse with her long, thin fingers. "By the time I am done with him, he will be begging me to look after all his affairs for him. I shall have control over his money, and he will be grateful for it. Because he will be too afraid of the world and life itself."

Like partners in crime, they both grinned at each other's reflection in the mirror. He bent over to kiss her in the neck, and she tilted her head slightly. His lips on her skin felt hot and passionate.

The more Josephine thought about it, the more their plan excited her. The solution to her problems had been so close, right under her nose in fact.

Looking at herself in the mirror, she let her gaze examine her own features. With every passing year, she grew to like less and less what she saw in the mirror. Every day, she would find another imperfection, another wrinkle, another grey hair.

But when she thought of the future that lay before her now, she felt invigorated. She imagined herself holding the spirits of the people around her in her hand like a delicate flower, to be crushed and destroyed forever at her own leisure. And with every soul flower she touched, the rose she believed inside her seemed to grow a new petal, another thorn.

When she thought of that power, she felt alive.

Chapter Eighteen

Nobody, including the servants, would have wanted to trade places with young Master Bosworth. Even Lily and Margaret seemed to take pity on him, because Stella hardly ever heard the two maids mocking the boy in private anymore. For hours on end, Alfie would be locked away in his father's study, which was now his own, while a parade of private tutors kept him busy. He wasn't told why he was made to work so hard, only that it was for his own good.

Watching him sitting at the breakfast table, he looked even more downtrodden than usual to Stella.

Gathering up his courage, he took a deep breath. "Mother," he asked, trying to sound as sweet as he possibly could, "I was wondering if I might be permitted to take Atlantis out for a short ride this afternoon. The weather is—"

"Certainly not," Mrs Bosworth cut him off. "You have more important matters to attend."

"But I am doing really well with my lessons, so I thought that perhaps you would allow me to take some fresh air?"

"You are doing well because you work hard. We cannot afford to dilute your efforts. And if it's fresh air you want, then open a window in your study."

"Even at boarding school pupils are allowed to be outside and have some time off," he pouted.

"Boarding school? I thought we had agreed boarding school wasn't right for you? You have all the best tutors here."

Haughtily, she brushed away a bread crumb from the tablecloth. "Besides, I know how much you dreaded going. And who could blame you, when your life here with me is so pleasant."

Pleasant, my foot, Stella thought.

"But I want to go, Mother," Alfie protested.

His mother's air of surprise fooled no one. "Why the sudden change of heart?"

"I would like to have friends, Mother. I am so dreadfully alone."

She clicked her tongue disapprovingly. "Nonsense! You have me, don't you? Or am I not good enough for you? Is that it, you petulant, ungrateful child?"

"I'm not–"

"Quiet," she interrupted sharply. "I will hear no more of your whining. It's not what I deserve after trying so hard to care for you all on my own, day after day. You will stay here at home, and that is final."

Alfie lowered his gaze. "Yes, Mother."

"And as for going out riding? Since you feel you have time for such frivolous activities, I shall instruct your tutors that they need to give you more work."

Stella could see his lower lip was beginning to tremble. *Don't cry, Alfie. Don't give her that pleasure.* Behind Mrs Bosworth's back, she shot her monstrous mistress an angry glare. She was seething on the inside.

And that rage only subsided many hours later, when she had a chance to tell her tale and blow off some steam at the stables with Pete.

"Want to have a go with this?" he asked, holding out his pitchfork to her.

"At that wretched woman, you mean? A tempting offer, but I think I'll have to pass. She isn't worth the trouble I'd get into if I attacked her with a pitchfork."

Pete laughed. "Not at her! At one of these, I meant." He indicated the stable boxes with a nod of his head. "Cleaning out the stables is good exercise. Makes you forget all your troubles."

Despite his friendly smile, his brown eyes looked at her with genuine concern, and she knew he would have hugged her if she let it happen.

"I will let you do the mucking out," she said. "But I'll be sure to remember your advice." Then, with a miserable sigh, she asked, "Is there any way we can help him?"

Pete thought about it for a while. "Unless you want to smuggle him out of the house and put him on a ship to America, I don't think there's much we can do."

Pursing his lips in frustration, he put his hands in his pockets. "She's his mother, and she's got that rat-faced Preston on her side. While our opinions, and our feelings, mean nothing in this world."

Stella let her shoulders sink. The longer she stayed at the Bosworth household, the more she was overcome with a feeling of powerlessness. It was like being locked in a room that grew smaller by the day, the walls closing in while your spirit slowly perished. The only escape was Pete. She feared that without him, her emotions would eat her up from the inside.

"We have to let him know we're here for him, Pete. If Alfie is unable to come to us to chat, then we have to find another way."

"Well, we certainly can't go to him, can we?"

"Not in person, no." She snapped her fingers as an idea struck her. "But our words could!"

"Eh?"

"We could slip him notes – or I could anyway, whenever I bring him his meals or refreshments. We could write something together."

Pete bit his lip. "*You* could write something, you mean." He sounded ashamed, which was a rare occurrence for him she thought.

"Oh," she said, as something dawned on her. "You can't read or write, can you?"

He shrugged, avoiding her gaze. "Knowing your numbers and letters isn't much use when you're a stable boy."

Instantly, she regretted having blurted out her question like that. She had embarrassed him. And Pete was the last person whom she wanted to cause any pain.

She flashed him an apologetic smile. "You might not be able to write, but you've got a way with words," she said encouragingly. "You make me laugh every day, and I've never heard anyone say smarter things about life than you."

"I still think you should write it," he smiled rather shyly. "You know how to make people feel better." He looked at her, his face suddenly serious. "Your words can heal hearts."

And so, she wrote her heart out for Alfie. Her words of comfort, combined with Pete's witty remarks and jests.

The next day, when she was asked to take some tea and biscuits to Alfie's study, she winked at him as she set down her tray. Following her gaze, he spotted the letter she had hidden underneath the teapot, and smiled.

Later, when she went to collect the tray again, she found his written reply and hid it up her sleeve.

In the evening, she went to the stables and read out Alfie's letter to Pete while the two of them sat on a bale of hay.

"*My dear friends,*

You cannot believe how happy I was to read your kind note. You are correct, at the moment I am unable to come visit you, even though I would love to do nothing more. I must study day and night, and Mother fears my education will be compromised by too much leisure time.

Sometimes, I look out of my window and I see the back wall of the mews behind the garden. Then I imagine Atlantis resting peacefully in his stable.

Oh, how I would love to be a horse!

I wouldn't mind having to carry someone on my back, if it meant I could run free through parks and over meadows.

Alas, I am not a horse. I am a lonely boy, and even more isolated now than when my father was still alive.

But I am glad to know my best friends are still thinking of me and that they care for me. Hopefully, one day we can be together again, playing cards and talking in the stables, like old times.

Until then, I wish you both the best.

Love,
Alfie"

Stella felt sad as she folded up the letter again.

Pete echoed her sentiments when he said, "Poor lad. 'Compromise his education' – ridiculous! The hag has got him firmly in her grip, and he doesn't even realise it."

"She's very good at making his life hell while pretending it's for his own good."

They sat there for a while, both thinking about their friend who was imprisoned by his own mother. Then Stella had an idea.

"What if we meet him here at night? We could each sneak to the stables after everyone has gone to sleep."

"That's risky though. Won't the other maids hear you?"

"Not if I'm careful." She had memories of silently moving through the shadows at the workhouse to escape the bullies. "I can be very quiet if I have to."

Hesitantly, Pete nodded. "If Alfie manages to be quiet too, it might work."

"It wouldn't have to be long. Just for a few moments, to take his mind off things and put a smile on his face. That would mean the world to him."

"Sounds like we have a plan then," he muttered, clearly not overly convinced.

But even with his skeptical approval, Stella was overjoyed. In her excitement, she wrapped her arms around his neck and kissed him on the cheek.

"Thank you," she said, smiling happily.

"Hey," he grinned. "Anything for you, right?"

"And for Alfie."

"Yeah," he replied, heaving himself up on his feet again with a groan. "For him too."

Chapter Nineteen

Through the windows of the country manor, Stella watched the leaves move and sway gently on the trees. In the cool summer breeze, they looked like green waves, rolling and dancing to their own rhythm. She longed to be out there, free to run between those trees. And beyond them she knew there lay pretty meadows of green grass that would feel so pleasingly fresh underneath her bare feet.

"Emma," Mrs Bosworth snapped.

With a startled jolt, Stella was snatched back to the reality of the moment. When she saw her mistress' nearly empty teacup, she cursed herself for not paying better attention.

"I'm sorry, ma'am," she said hastily, and hurried to refill the cup.

"Sleeping is something you do in your bed at night, you brainless ninny. Not while you are serving breakfast."

"Yes, ma'am. Sorry, ma'am," Stella mumbled as she stepped away from the table again. In her years as a maid for the Bosworths, she had uttered those words of apology so often that they had lost any meaning. They were simply sounds one produced when the mistress was displeased.

"Anyway," the lady of the house said, dismissing both the matter and Stella already, while returning her focus to her two table companions. "Today promises to be a good day to go for a little ride, don't you think, Charles?"

"The weather does indeed appear quite pleasant," Mr Preston nodded with a smile. "Do you care to join us, Alfie? Make it a little family outing, eh? I'm sure Atlantis would be glad to see you again. What do you say, lad?"

But Alfie remained silent, like he so often did these days. His former joy for riding and the country estate had disappeared. Stella noticed that he had barely touched his breakfast this morning. He seemed distant, as if in his mind he was somewhere else.

"Alfred!" Mrs Bosworth yelled angrily. "Answer the man."

Alfie stared at his mother with eyes that were glassy, making Stella wonder if he had actually heard anything of the things said before.

"Yes, Mr Preston," he replied in a tone of voice that was devoid of any joy, any emotion, and even, life. He sounded like he was dead inside, Stella thought with a heavy heart.

"Splendid," his mother chirped. "I'll have the servants prepare a luncheon for us, so we can have a picnic. Won't that be lovely, darling?"

She and Mr Preston both looked at Alfie, waiting for him to reciprocate their enthusiasm. But the sad, soulless boy merely pushed the food on his plate around a bit with his fork.

"Alfie?" Mr Preston said with a warning tone in his voice. "Your mother asked you a question."

"Yes, Mother," he replied perfunctorily.

"Honestly, Alfie," Mrs Bosworth sighed. "I don't know what has got into you lately. Must you always be this recalcitrant?"

"Sorry, Mother."

Don't be sorry, Alfie, Stella wanted to scream. *Speak your mind, and tell her to leave you in peace for a change!*

But she knew all too well he would never dare to do that. He wasn't strong enough to stand up to his mother's ever-changing moods and demands.

And the way Mrs Bosworth had been treating her son, he wasn't getting any stronger either.

Which, Stella was beginning to suspect, was probably the whole idea.

"You could at least pretend to be a little excited about spending time with your Mother," Mrs Bosworth said, sounding hurt.

Alfie forced a smile onto his face, and politely nodded at his mother. It was a saddening display of well-trained obedience that made Stella want to cry.

"May I be excused?" he asked.

"Of course," Mr Preston replied.

"Make sure you're ready to leave in one hour," Mrs Bosworth added.

Alfie nodded to them both with a straight face, got up and left the room. Stella wanted to follow him, to talk to him, just so he would hear a couple of friendly words as well this morning. But she had to remain at her station until breakfast was over and the room had been cleared.

As soon as she could, she went over to his room, under the pretence of bringing him some clean towels. Looking around to check no one else was around, she gave a quick knock on his door.

"Not now," a groan sounded from inside.

"Alfie, it's me," she whispered. "Do you want to talk?"

After a pause, he said, "I'm not in the mood right now." Stella couldn't see his tears, but she heard them in his voice. It trembled, betraying his fear and confusion.

She sighed. "We'll be in the stables tonight if you need us."

"I know."

She hesitated by his door, desperate to help her friend, realising all too well there wasn't much more she could do.

Alfie's behaviour worried her. Despite their secret late-night meetings at the stables, she and Pete couldn't keep his spirits up. Even when he was near the horses with them, Alfie didn't talk as much as he used to, and a general air of sadness had taken hold of his face and body. Whatever they tried, it didn't seem to cheer the boy up.

Stella was frustrated about her own powerlessness. And she was angry at the wickedness of Mrs Bosworth and Mr Preston. It was almost as if they got pleasure from pushing the boy around.

With a mind full of dark and conflicting thoughts, Stella returned to the large kitchen before Mrs Burch could chastise her for taking too long. But instead of the austere housekeeper, she found Lily and Margaret whispering and giggling among each other. Young Esther was sitting with the older maids as well.

"Have you seen how pale and frightened he looked?" Lily asked her two friends.

"Yes, Mother," Margaret mocked in a high-pitched voice. "Sorry, Mr Preston." The girls laughed at her impression.

So they were talking about Alfie, Stella understood straight away.

"They've tamed him better than any of the horses," Lily giggled.

"That's because he takes after his fathead father," Margaret said. She crossed her eyes and puffed up her cheeks, sending the other two girls into a fit of hysterical laughter.

Stella's blood started boiling. "You chattering hens better stop your gossiping," she hissed. "You should be ashamed of yourselves talking about Alfie like that. And you, Esther, shouldn't you be scrubbing dishes in the scullery?"

She was particularly disappointed about the young girl sitting with these two serpents. Esther wasn't the brightest, but she had seemed kind so far. Stella didn't want the scullery maid to come under the nasty influence of Lily and Margaret.

But her words had the opposite effect.

"Oh, look everyone," Lily sneered. "It's Princess Stella."

Margaret and Esther covered their mouths to hide their mocking laughter.

"What's wrong, Princess Stella?" Lily asked. "Did your prince not want to kiss you this morning?"

Margaret made kissing noises at Stella. "I bet they do more than kiss when he invites her into his room, you know?"

"Shut your filthy mouth," Stella growled. "Or I'll—"

"Or you will what?" Lily challenged her.

"Careful, Lily," Margaret said, pretending to be afraid. "She might run to the mistress, to tell her we've been saying bad things about their precious Alfred."

"Yeah?" Lily replied with an evil smile on her face. "Well, then she'd better also tell the mistress about those secret meetings she's been having at the stables."

Stella's eyes grew wide. They knew about that?

"Did you see her reaction, girls?" Lily said to her friends. "She's guilty as sin!"

Margaret and Esther grinned.

"Of course we know about your late-night encounters, you silly tart," Lily continued. "Carrying on with a stable boy *and* the heir of the manor? Very naughty."

"What?!" Stella was furious about such an outrageous lie. "I'm not carrying on with anyone."

"Pull the other one, girl," Lily laughed. She raised her skirts to show her left leg, and then dangled it playfully.

Joining in the mockery, Margaret turned round and stuck out her rear. "I've been a very naughty pony," she giggled. "Alfie, Pete, somebody please punish me."

She smacked her own bottom, and the other two girls nearly doubled over with laughter.

In a blind rage, Stella flew at her to put a stop to this distasteful and slanderous spectacle. But Lily stepped in and grabbed hold of Stella's arms.

"What's the matter, Princess?" she snarled. "Can't handle the truth?"

"It's not the truth," Stella said through gritted teeth. "It's a dirty lie."

Still holding her by the arms, Lily leaned in closer and spat Stella in the face. "The only thing dirty here is you, you filthy slattern."

The older maid gave her a violent shove, sending her flying backwards. Stella stumbled and fell on the hard kitchen floor. The back of her head hit the ground, sending a blinding flash of pain through her skull.

Picking herself up again, she saw Lily and Margaret laughing viciously at her. Esther seemed a bit unsure, because her eyes darted between Stella and the other two maids. But then she threw in her lot with the older girls, and decided to laugh along.

"What's all this commotion about?" the stern voice of Mrs Burch demanded.

"Stella tried to assault me, Mrs Burch," Margaret blurted out.

"That's right," Lily said. "She didn't like us telling her off for disappearing right after breakfast. Left us to do most of the work, she did."

"Is that so?" the housekeeper replied, peering at Stella suspiciously. "Consider this your fair warning then, Miss Reed. I shan't tolerate any loafing about or anyone shirking their duties. Nor will I accept violent behaviour among the staff."

Knowing it was useless to argue, Stella fled the kitchen – with Mrs Burch's gaze burning in her back and the maids' scornful laughter ringing painfully in her ears. As bitter tears came to her eyes, memories of the workhouse haunted her mind. How often had she been cornered there, with the other children calling her names, before they proceeded to rough her up?

She had hoped with all her heart that working in the Bosworth household would stop the bullying. And that her position as a maid would herald the beginning of a new life.

But now it turned out nothing had really changed.

It wasn't fair! What had she ever done to anyone to deserve this?

Angry and crying, she left the main house and crossed the yard towards the stables. Pete had just the cure for her current state of mind, she knew.

Chapter Twenty

Stella rushed through the open doors of the stables. Upon spotting Pete, she marched straight at him, her face determined and unsmiling.

"Stella," he said, surprised to see her at the stables at this time of day. He could tell something was wrong.

She didn't say anything to him however. She simply grabbed the pitchfork from his hands and stomped past him, into one of the empty stable boxes. Furiously, she started digging into the straw with the pitchfork.

She didn't know what to do and she was too angry to care, so she just stabbed at the bedding and threw the straw around. With every thrust, she imagined Lily, Margaret or any of her past bullies to be hiding underneath that thick layer. And every swing of the pitchfork felt like she was ridding herself of another tormenting spectre from her life.

Her movements were wild and erratic, so Pete wisely decided to stand back and let her rage for as long as she wanted. Her frantic shovelling sent up clouds of dust and straw into the air, but she was too upset to worry about her clothes getting dirty.

After a few minutes of pure madness, her arms started getting tired and her mind began to calm down somewhat. She stabbed at her imaginary opponents a few more times, and then stopped.

As the dust slowly settled around her, she wiped the sweat off her brow with her sleeve. Her racing heart was beating wildly in her chest, and she could feel the pulsating veins in her head.

Stella turned to Pete, who still stood staring at her with a bewildered look on his face.

"You were right," she panted, almost happily. "Working in the stables does clear your mind. I feel better already."

Coming out of the box, she handed him back his pitchfork.

"I'm glad," Pete said, suppressing a grin. "But you just tossed up a perfectly clean box."

Her spirits sank. "Oh no," she apologised, anxiously looking back at the mess she had created. "I'm so sorry." Her tears were threatening to return. "I didn't– I only wanted–"

"Don't worry," he smiled. "It's okay. It won't take long to tidy it up again."

"Here, let me," she said quickly while trying to take his pitchfork.

"No, thank you," he teased, keeping it away from her. "You've done enough, I should think."

He had meant it as a joke, but she started crying again and hid her face in her hands. Immediately, he stepped up to her and put an arm around her.

"Stella, what's wrong?" he asked, full of concern. "What happened?" She was shaking in his arms.

"The girls in the kitchen," she replied, wiping her runny nose. "They were making fun of Alfie, so I told them off. And then they accused me of... slanderous things. So I got angry."

She sniffed and continued, "I didn't hurt anyone, but they threw me on the floor. And now Mrs Burch thinks *I'm* the idle troublemaker."

"Sounds like you've had quite an eventful morning already," Pete said.

"I just got so mad at them for speaking ill of Alfie. He's in so much pain lately, Pete. I can't bear to see him suffer like that."

Pete studied her face carefully, and she smelled the comforting scent of his body. It calmed her. Being close to Pete always had that effect on her. When he was around, the world made more sense to her.

But when he wasn't... Well, things had a tendency to fall apart then.

After a brief silence, he sighed. "Why are you risking your reputation and your job for the rich son of the family?" he asked her calmly, but firmly.

What? She blinked her eyes.

"Because he is my friend," she threw back at him vehemently, as if he had just asked her why she loved her mother. "And yours too, in case you'd forgotten."

"Stella, I don't know how much more I have to tell you this, but he will never be our friend.

It's only a matter of time until we do something to upset him. And then you and I will be the ones left to deal with the consequences."

"But don't you see! We're the only people he has. He's cut off from any other boys, he doesn't seem to have young relatives, his mother won't let him go to boarding school, and he's barely allowed to visit his horses anymore."

Stella talked fast, intent on telling Pete all her arguments before she forgot them. Or before he tried to change her mind. "Who is his friend if not us?"

She searched his face for clues.

But he merely shook his head.

"I know he's an unfortunate, unhappy boy, Stella. He's lonely, I get that. But that doesn't matter. We're risking our livelihoods by humouring him. Every time we sneak out to see him, every time we write him a letter, and every time we arrange one of our meetings, we could lose our jobs and get kicked out."

Taking her by the sides of her shoulders, he shook her lightly. "Heck, you've just told me you got in trouble with the maids, *and* Mrs Burch, over standing up for the boy!"

He was talking himself into a rage now. "And what for, Stella? I know you pity him, we all do. But it's not worth the risk, do you hear?"

She stared at him with her mouth half open in disbelief.

Calming himself again, he put a friendly hand on her shoulder. "Do you know what punishment he would get for breaking the rules? A slap on the wrist, that's all."

Irritated, she shook off his hand from her shoulder.

But he didn't let up. "Maybe he'd get told to stay in his room for a week. He'll still have his fortune and his horses and his parties just the same. But what about us, Stella?"

"What about us?" she asked angrily.

"The likes of us stand to lose everything when things go wrong. Nobody would look out for us. Which is why we need to look out for ourselves."

Stella glared at him. "Nice speech," she scoffed. "So what do you propose we do then? Nothing? Are we just supposed to desert him? Left to the mercy of his wicked mother and soon-to-be stepfather, who would gladly crush him under their heel?"

Her heart grew heavy at the thought of it. "Do you realise how happy I would have been to have had someone to help me when I most needed it?"

Speaking of it brought tears to her eyes again. "Day and night, I prayed for an angel to save me from that horrible workhouse, and from the bullies who tormented and beat me. I was so terribly alone. I had no one."

He looked away from her, but now it was her turn to not let up. "I was grateful the nightmare finally ended when Mrs Bosworth hired me as a maid. Even though it meant the beginning of another nightmare."

She grabbed his sleeve, making him look her in the eye again. "So if you think I'm going to abandon a friend who needs our support, then you are terribly mistaken, Pete Draper."

She stared at him intensely, and he stared back. Clenching his jaw, she saw that he was struggling with his emotions. But then he swallowed his pride and relaxed his face.

"I didn't know you had it so rough at the workhouse," he said, his voice slightly hoarse. "I'm sorry to hear that."

Stella said nothing.

"And I'm sorry if I reacted a bit strong," he continued. "It's because of my father, I think."

"Your father?"

Pete nodded. "He always taught me to keep my distance. 'Don't become too attached,' he would tell me. 'Don't let anyone get too close to your heart.'"

"That's just sad, Pete. Why would he do that?"

"When they were young, his brother fell in love with the daughter of the master he was working for, and he was fired for it. We haven't seen my uncle ever since. Last thing we heard he went to Germany. I think my father's afraid of losing me too."

Lost in his thoughts, Pete bit his lower lip. Then he looked at Stella again, his brown eyes moist with emotion.

"And I'm afraid of losing you," he said.

His words felt like they reached down into her chest and touched her in the very centre of her heart. She took his face in her hands, unable to say anything. He responded by gently touching one of her hands with his.

"Promise me you'll be careful," he begged her.

"I will," she said quietly.

"Promise me I won't lose you."

As Pete said that, only inches away from her face, she was convinced she had never seen a kinder and more beautiful person than him.

"I promise," she whispered.

Slowly, she moved her face closer to his... until their lips touched.

Chapter Twenty-One

Returning to the crowded, smelly city after spending the summer months in the lush openness of the countryside always felt dull. But this year, the transition was even harder for Stella. In the past, Alfie would go home with renewed energy and good humour. This time however, the fresh air and green landscapes had borne no fruits. He looked sickly pale at the end of summer, since he hardly went outside during their stay. And his mother had done absolutely nothing to entice him to enjoy the good weather or the healthy outdoors.

Stella and Pete hadn't been able to meet with him for weeks, even though she waited at the stables after work almost every night, in case their friend did decide to come over.

To make matters worse, this tense waiting situation did nothing to improve the relationship between her and Pete. Despite that one and only brief moment of passion, their friendship hadn't had much chance to evolve further.

And he still had his reservations about getting too close to Alfie. Which caused some unspoken friction between them every time she came over to the stables in the hope of seeing Alfie – so far, in vain.

Then one night, her luck changed however. Because their young friend finally came through the underground tunnel into the mews.

"Alfie," Stella exclaimed happily. "You came!" She ran to throw her arms around him. He hugged her back, though reluctantly.

"It's good to be here, Stella."

His voice sounded raspy, and Stella couldn't tell if it was because of his strict and secluded lifestyle, or because his voice had begun to mature.

Pete watched them from a corner of the stables, casually leaning against a stack of hay. His apparent lack of enthusiasm didn't escape Stella.

"Come say hello, Pete," she urged him.

He merely crossed his arms and said, "Hello."

Stella frowned at him. She understood the reason for his cool behaviour, but it still irritated her that he would choose to be this stubborn and not show some more kindness to Alfie, who – thankfully – didn't seem to notice.

"You won't believe how much I've missed you two," the boy said, as he sat down on a stool. He rubbed his face, looking exhausted. "I swear this rigorous schedule my mother has devised will finish me off some day."

"Well, we're here to make sure that doesn't happen," Stella promised. "Isn't that so, Pete?"

A mumbling noise was all the reply she got from him. Choosing to ignore his funny mood, she sat down next to Alfie.

"After all," she smiled, "we wouldn't know what to do around here without you."

Reluctantly, Pete finally decided to join them.

"I'm fairly sure I would," he said. "Work keeps me busy for most of the day." There wasn't any trace of his usual good humour in his voice.

Confusion plainly visible on his face, Alfie looked from Stella to Pete and back again. "What's going on?"

"Nothing, nothing," Stella said hastily. "Nothing you need to worry about." She flashed him a quick smile, but it felt forced.

"Merely a difference of opinion," Pete added.

Alfie seemed relieved at that reply. "Good," he said happily. "Because look what I've brought you."

He placed a large folded napkin on his lap and opened it, revealing an assortment of little cakes and pastries.

" I stole them from the dinner table," he giggled. "They're for you." Proudly and carefully, he picked up the napkin with both hands and held it out to them. "Here, help yourselves."

Pete and Stella devoured the dessert in minutes, making them forget about their own little squabble for a moment.

"Thanks, Alfie," Pete said, licking the last crumbs off his fingers. "It's a shame delicious stuff like this doesn't reach the servants' table more often."

"It does," Stella pointed out. "Just not our end of the table. I've seen the housekeeper and the butler eat this sort of thing before. They often seem to get better food than the rest of us."

"Yeah, well, they can keep their fancy food. I wouldn't want to have to wear a uniform every day like they do. Scurrying around like a mouse, kissing the feet of Mrs Bosworth."

"A uniform is just a set of clothes," Stella shrugged. "You get used to it. And as for kissing Mrs Bosworth's feet? I suppose we don't all enjoy the peace and freedom of the stables. Some of us have to be polite and nod, and put up with unpleasant people."

Alfie shifted on his stool, and she could see their argument was making him uncomfortable.

"But let's not bore Alfie with our tedious niggles," she said. "What have you been up to, Alfie?"

"I don't mind listening to you two really," he replied. "I don't feel much like talking lately."

With some effort, Stella brought the conversation to the summer they had just spent in the countryside. Knowing he was a born storyteller, she prodded Pete to reminisce about the precious few fun moments they had spent together.

And soon, Alfie was laughing at the memories and at the way Pete could spin a tale out of the smallest detail.

After about half an hour, he got up and smiled, "It's been splendid and it has done me a world of good, my dear friends. But now I must go. See you soon?"

"See you soon," Stella answered, grateful to see him restored like this.

"Yeah, don't be a stranger," Pete winked.

After they had watched him disappear into the underground tunnel that led back to the house, a silence fell between the two of them. There was so much to say and discuss, but no time to do it in.

"I'd better go too," she said quietly. "It's late."

He nodded, staring at his shoes.

Then he looked at her, and with a mute apology in his eyes, he gently took her hands. "See you soon?"

"See you soon," she replied, willing yet unable to say more. She smiled at him, and he smiled back at her.

Moving away from him, their fingers slipped away from each other. She forced herself to walk towards the tunnel. She would rather have run back to him, to hug him and to feel his lips again, while they whispered sweet words of tenderness to each other.

But she couldn't. She mustn't. Not now.

Her mind and her heart locked in a battle, she walked through the darkened tunnel. Alfie would be back in the house by now, she assumed. They certainly couldn't afford to be seen coming out of the tunnel together.

A frightened shriek at the other end made her stop dead in her tracks. That had sounded like Alfie!

"Mother, I can explain," she thought she heard him cry.

No, her mind shouted in fear. *He's been caught by his mother!*

Leaning flat against the wall in the shadows of the tunnel, she listened in on the unfolding drama.

"There's nothing to explain," Mrs Bosworth growled like a tiger about to attack her prey. "I try to provide the best possible care and education for you, Alfred Bosworth. But here you are ruining your health by prowling around in the middle of the night."

"I– I couldn't sleep," Alfie stammered. "So I decided to get out of bed to stretch my legs."

Stella heard a smacking sound and another shriek from Alfie.

"And you came all the way to those filthy stables for that? You liar!"

"Mother, I wasn't–"

"Silence! I have had enough of your lies, your excuses and your awful behaviour. You are an ungrateful boy and you need to learn your lesson once and for all."

"Mother, you're hurting me," he whimpered. "Please let go, I beg you."

"I will let you go if you march up those stairs," Mrs Bosworth barked. "From now on, you are not to leave your room without my explicit permission. No visitors either. Your tutors will escort you to your study."

Stella heard stumbling noises and another cry of pain from Alfie. She gathered Mrs Bosworth was shoving her son towards the stairs.

"And as for that foul-smelling horse of yours," Mrs Bosworth shouted. "Pray I don't send him off to the glue factory!"

"Mother, no!"

"Then go to your room and obey your mother."

Their voices trailed off, as they went up the stairs with Mrs Bosworth hurtling further threats and abuse at her son.

In the darkness, Stella breathed a sigh of relief that she hadn't been caught with Alfie. That would have made matters a thousand times worse. For both of them, no doubt.

She rushed back towards the mews. Because she didn't want to risk being discovered, and she needed to speak to Pete. He had to calm the sheer panic in her mind.

Chapter Twenty-Two

Stella ran straight into Pete's arms. He was surprised and glad to see her, but her sudden return and her agitated behaviour betrayed something was terribly wrong.

"What happened?" he asked, hugging her close to him. "You seem like you watched someone getting murdered."

"She nearly did if you ask me," Stella said, still pressing the side of her face close to his chest.

"Who did?"

"Mrs Bosworth. She must have caught Alfie coming out of the tunnel. I heard her screaming and ranting at him."

"Did she see you?" Pete asked immediately.

"No, I don't think so. I stayed in the dark, and she was too focused on Alfie."

"Thank goodness for that," he sighed.

"But Pete, don't you see?" She let go of him and looked up, her eyes intense and urgent. "We have to help him!"

"Calm down, Stella," he told her gently. "Alfie got caught by his mother, and now she's angry with him. But you weren't implicated, so you're safe."

"Yes, but he isn't!"

"Alfie will be fine. She's going to come up with some kind of punishment, and it'll all be forgotten in a few weeks. Or until the next bit of drama presents itself."

"Not this time, Pete," she shook her head. "She was furious. You should have heard her. She said he wasn't allowed to leave his room anymore without her permission."

"That doesn't sound too bad to me," he chuckled. "It's not the first time he's been told to stay in his room."

"I'm telling you this is different, Pete!"

He raised his hands. "Okay, so this is different."

"She can't do this to him." Her voice was quivering with fear and outrage. "She cannot possibly keep him a prisoner in his own room forever!"

"In all the time you've been here," Pete replied, "have you ever known one thing that woman was incapable of doing? She's like an all-powerful goddess in this household, in case you hadn't noticed."

Pouting angrily, Stella paced up and down.

"Her word is law," Pete continued. "And her wish is our command."

"I know, I know. But that doesn't mean I have to like it. Or even accept it. Pete, there has to be a way to stop her."

Sneering sarcastically, he said, "Have you ever tried to stop the rain from falling, or lighting from striking? That woman is a force of nature, Stella. The best we can do is to try and avoid her."

She glared at him. "Since when have you become such a coward?"

"I beg your pardon?"

"All this talk about goddesses and forces of nature. She's made of flesh and blood, just like us. She's human, and so are we. There must be something we can do."

"Heavens above, you sound like you were born yesterday," he groaned. "Of course she's a human being just like the rest of us. But that doesn't mean she's the same. Blood may flow through her veins, she needs to eat and sleep, and like any other mortal, she'll die and rot away some day."

He took her by her arms and looked her straight in the eye. "But Stella, that doesn't matter. What separates the likes of her from the likes of us is fancy clothes, money and power. And those things make a world of difference."

She turned her face away so she wouldn't have to meet his gaze. "Don't you think I know that?" She pushed back the tears she felt coming on.

"I know that you know. But do you really understand what it means? They are our masters, Stella. And we are their slaves."

"We aren't slaves," she protested, sounding less convinced than she wanted.

"Aren't we? She can hurt you, or treat you however badly as she wishes, and there isn't a thing you can say or do about it. Because if you did, you'd end up on the street without any references. You'd be back in the workhouse in no time."

Impassioned, he shook her a little. "She doesn't even bother to call you by your name,

Stella. You are not a person to her. You're a worthless servant who has no choice but to cater to her every whim. Something for her to boss around. And that will never change, not in a thousand years."

Stella struggled to free herself from his grip. "I don't care how she treats me. As long as Alfie can be happy," she blurted out. "I can deal with the abuse. I'm used to insults and beatings. The workhouse saw to that."

He let her go, and she turned her back to him. "I could be happy here, even as a servant working for a cruel mistress. As long as I have you and Alfie as a friend."

She wrapped her arms around her body, rubbing herself slowly with her hands.

Pete sighed. "Stella, I–"

"You're right," she cut him off bitterly. "Mrs Bosworth is not like us at all. But you have to agree she can't treat her son like that, not even with all the power she has!"

"And yet, she does," he said sadly. "Many things in this world aren't right, or fair. But they happen all the same."

With hot tears running down her face, she spun back round at him and nearly shrieked, "Well, I won't stand for such injustice!"

"Ah, brave little Stella," he smirked, growing impatient. "Willing to sacrifice all she has, to defend her naive notions. And dragging others down with her in the process, mind. But what for?"

He pointed in the direction of the main house, and struck a denouncing tone, "For a boy who won't even remember your name the day he moves out of his mother's house!"

"How dare you?" she hissed. "You know he's not like that. He's not like his mother. Alfie is caring and sweet, and he genuinely loves us. He's our friend!"

"No, Stella," Pete replied, very calm and determined all of a sudden. "He can never be our friend. We've been kind to him, but we've also been putting ourselves in danger because of that kindness."

"And yet Alfie is the one who's in trouble right now! Not us."

"Not yet anyway. His mother is bound to wonder if anyone was with him on his little outing here. And guess who'll be her prime suspect then?"

He pointed at himself with an angry thumb. "Me."

Lifting her chin defiantly, she taunted, "I didn't realise you were such a craven coward, Pete Draper."

"Stop calling me a coward," he warned her. "You know I can't be his friend. It's too dangerous."

Studying his tensed face, she could tell those words pained him. But she was too angry to care.

"Maybe it's for the best that you're not his friend then," she said, swallowing her tears. "Maybe you ought to stay away from troublemakers like me as well. Before you expose yourself to any more risks or dangers."

The glare she shot him was cold and scornful. "Friendship isn't worth your prestigious position as a stable boy after all."

"Fine!" he blew up. "Insult me all you want. You go ahead and be friends with the little master. Maybe one day he'll run away with you and make you his wife, like in those books you like." He gesticulated wildly with his arms. "Then you can spend the rest of your days making the love of your life a happy man."

"What?! I'm not in love with him," she cried.

"But it sure sounds like it," he argued bitterly. "Why else would you be willing to throw away our friendship? Or whatever it is that you and I had between us."

"Is that what this is about, Pete?" She couldn't believe what she was hearing. "Are you jealous? Because I want to stand up for a poor, terrorised boy?"

"That's all who you care for," he shot back at her.

"You don't possibly believe that, do you?"

"If you cared the least bit about me, you would listen to me!"

"I am listening to you," she fumed. "But you're talking nothing but nonsense and rubbish. Why must you be so selfish?"

He fell silent, and Stella used the brief pause to catch her breath from all their angry yelling. Her head was pounding with the raging emotions that were bouncing around.

"Ah yes, of course," Pete said sarcastically. "I'm selfish for protecting you." He inhaled deeply. "I should've known from the start, I suppose. But instead, I enabled all of this. I'm the one who allowed you to have your secret meetings here."

Dramatically shoving his hands in his pockets, he scoffed, "How foolish of me to think you would want to spend your time with someone as selfish as me."

"I thought you were better than this, Pete," she said, shaking her head sadly.

"I guess you were wrong then."

"It would appear so," she answered, pulling up one side of her mouth in a sorry smile. Slowly, she turned around, in the direction of the tunnel door.

"Goodbye, Pete."

The words were soft, and seemingly emotionless, although there lay an ocean of sorrow and heartbreak beyond them.

"That's right," he called after her. "Leave! But don't think you can come running back to me next time Mrs Meanworth treats you like a rag. Or when the other maids call you all sorts of names again."

Keeping her back straight and her head high, Stella walked towards the underground tunnel to the house. As she closed the door behind her, the act felt horribly final.

Right after the door had shut, she heard a curse escape from Pete's lips, and a loud thud when he kicked at a stable wall in anger.

Grateful for the silent darkness surrounding her, she started walking the long and lonely way to her room.

Chapter Twenty-Three

Stella hardly slept a wink the following days. The tiny amount of sleep she did get was deeply troubled by repeated visions of what had happened that night at the stables. The night she had lost not one, but two friends. The only two friends she had in this cruel world.

Restless, she tossed and turned, causing her modest sleeping pallet to creak in the quiet night. So rather than risk waking the two women with whom she had to share the small attic room, she decided to lie still and stare at the ceiling instead, breathing in the stale and dusty air that smelled of the old wood in the floors and ceiling.

She was faintly aware of the hunger that rumbled in her stomach. But her appetite had deserted her ever since that dreadful night. She couldn't bear the thought of eating food. Having to sit at the same table as Pete was bad enough. The two of them didn't speak a word to each other during meals, and they took great care to avoid meeting each other's eyes.

Pete hadn't been his usual jovial and talkative self at the table, and Stella wondered if maybe that was a good sign? Did it mean he too was feeling bad about the harsh words that had been spoken? Or was it merely because he continued to be angry with her?

Their behaviour hadn't escaped the attention of the other staff unfortunately. Which of course led to more gossip and speculation. Lily and Margaret in particular seemed to study Stella's every move and every hastily averted gaze. Their constant whispering and giggling at her expense nearly drove her insane.

But she needed to be careful now. With no more friends in this household, she could ill afford to create any more enemies. So she let Lily and Margaret laugh and gossip all they wanted, hoping they would grow bored with her, sooner or later, and find another victim to taunt instead.

A soft growling noise in her tummy brought her thoughts back to the cramped attic room she was lying in. Somewhat perversely, she rather enjoyed the dull, gnawing pain in her belly. Because it helped to distract her mind from the maddening hurt she experienced in her broken heart.

Without Pete and Alfie to talk to, the Bosworth residence felt like a dungeon to her. A dark place that sucked all the joy out of her, and where she was doomed to spend the rest of her miserable days. Despite the busy activities of the many people who lived and worked in the servants' quarters like her, she was utterly lonely.

Because except for nosy busybodies like Lily and Margaret, most of the staff were too caught up in their own misery to care about any of their colleagues. Envy and mistrust were rife. In the hard world below stairs, it was each man and woman to themselves.

And after her falling out with Pete, the house seemed colder than ever before.

Unable to sleep, she sighed and carefully tried to turn to one side, so she could stare at the moon-lit window instead of the dark ceiling for a change. The move made her feel the slight bulge in her thin mattress.

More memories, she grimaced.

Knowing all too well what was causing that bulge, she reached underneath the mattress and retrieved a leather-bound book.

It was the last book Alfie had managed to give her, before he got locked away into his room by his mother.

Absentmindedly stroking the luxurious cover with her hand, she thought back to their little book lending scheme, and smiled. It had been Alfie's idea of course, delighted as he was to discover that, finally, someone else in the house shared his love of reading.

She had already forgotten what the story of this particular book was about, but she remembered Alfie being quite fond of it.

"It's really great if you want to forget everything that makes you feel bad for a while," he had said when he gave it to her.

It would need to be a book with magic spells to have that effect on her now, she thought sorrowfully.

Closing her eyes, she breathed in the aromas of the book and then pressed it close to her chest.

In her mind, she could still see Alfie's face the day she had first met him. His cheeks round and rosy, his friendly eyes twinkling with kindness and excitement.

But what would he look like now, she wondered?

Nowhere near as happy, that much was for sure. Knowing how sensitive he was, she imagined him putting on a brave face while trying to hide the sadness inside. He would also be doing his utmost best to be an obedient son to his mother, and a committed pupil to his tutors. But at what price? His own health and happiness, no doubt.

Stella's heart skipped a beat when one of the other girls stirred in her sleep. Quickly, she hid the book underneath her blanket. The soft sound of peaceful snoring soon filled the room once more, and Stella sighed with relief.

She realised she needed to return the book soon. Books were expensive – especially finely crafted copies like the ones in the Bosworth library – and she couldn't risk someone finding it in her possession. There would be awkward questions, and then, even more awkward consequences.

Smuggling it back into Alfie's room had become a formidable challenge however. To begin with, the book was too big and too heavy for her to conceal on her person during the day. So she couldn't carry it with her all the time, in the hope that a suitable opportunity would arise to return it discreetly.

And under the current circumstances, those opportunities had only grown more rare. She didn't dare sneak up to his room without a perfectly good excuse, for fear of his mother or one of his tutors being with him.

She'd had only one chance to knock on his door so far, when she was passing by on her way back from one of the other rooms. But there had been no response. Either because he wasn't in his room – or perhaps because he didn't want to speak to anyone.

Maybe she should hide the book in the kitchen, she considered. Cook was bound to ask her to take up a meal to his room eventually. Then she could slip the book underneath the tray and return it to him. Even if he wasn't alone in his room, she could simply put down the tray on his table with the book under it.

No, she thought, dismissing the idea as too risky.

Or should she simply leave the book behind somewhere in the main house? As if someone had laid it down on a side table or a chair, and then forgotten about it?

But again, there were downsides to that plan. If Mrs Bosworth found the book lying around, she would suspect Alfie had left it there, since he was the only one in the house who read books. She would accuse him of being careless and untidy, and possibly punish him for it. Stella didn't want that on her conscience.

She would just have to wait for the right opportunity to come along. For now, she had to continue hiding the book.

As she slipped it back underneath her mattress, her hand knocked into something else. Something hard and cold to the touch. She knew what it was the moment she grabbed it to pull it out: the horseshoe Pete had given her as a lucky charm and as a memento of their first summer in the country.

How fitting that it had belonged to Atlantis, Alfie's favourite horse that Pete spent so much time caring for. The perfect symbol, connecting her to both of her friends.

Former friends, a dark voice in her head said.

Like she had done with Alfie's book, she ran her fingers over Pete's gift as well, blindly feeling the smooth metal surface and the holes where the horseshoe had been nailed to Atlantis' hoof.

She hesitated, slightly embarrassed, then brought the shoe close to her nose and sniffed at it tentatively.

It didn't smell of much, she was disappointed to note. She had expected a whiff of metal and horse, and secretly, or rather foolishly, she had hoped to detect the scent of Pete.

She smiled when she thought back to the day he had given her the horseshoe. How different their lives had seemed! They were servants, just like they still were now. But back then, they had been happy. Because they had their friendship to keep them going.

And they had kissed. She remembered that too.

Where had they gone wrong? What exactly had caused this rift between them? Why couldn't things return to the way they were?

Thinking about him pained her even more than thinking about Alfie. While Alfie was locked away out of sight, she saw Pete every day. Sometimes he was barely an arm's length away from her – so close physically, yet out of reach in several other ways.

She would love nothing more than to talk to him, but her pride kept her from taking the first step. She would not go back on what she said. She cared about Alfie and would find a way to help him.

A silent tear rolled down her cheek, and she quickly wiped it away with her hand.

No matter from which angle she looked at the situation, she couldn't bring herself to see any hope. Nor an easy way out.

Pete was right, she knew. Mrs Bosworth was indeed like an all-powerful, all-consuming evil force of nature. She was a destructive thunderstorm, and Stella was a leaf in the wind.

But would this storm die down and dwindle over time? Or would it first claim more helpless victims?

Chapter Twenty-Four

Stella looked on with surprise and disgust, as Mrs Bosworth put a third spoonful of sugar in her tea. She knew the mistress only ever did that whenever she was feeling particularly bored. Or frustrated.

The small silver spoon stirred through the teacup rapidly and noisily, which confirmed Stella's suspicion that something was troubling her employer. She made a mental note to be extra careful. In case *she* became the unfortunate subject of Mrs Bosworth's anger again.

With a short sigh, the lady of the house picked up one of the biscuits Cook had just made, and took a modest nibble from it. But immediately, she stared at it as if the biscuit had personally insulted her. Rolling her eyes irritably, she threw the offending treat back onto the tray.

Such revolting wastefulness, Stella tutted silently. She could smell the delicious aroma of the freshly baked biscuits from where she was standing. So she was sure there was absolutely nothing wrong with them.

But the mistress is always right, she reminded herself. *It doesn't concern you. Do your job, stay out of trouble, and get through another day.*

That was Stella's motto now. It wasn't much. But it helped her to survive in a household where she had no more friends.

With one eyebrow raised in displeasure, Mrs Bosworth picked up her cup. But as soon as she took one sip of her tea, she pulled a disgusted face.

"This is much too sweet," she complained while setting the cup down again. "Emma, what have you done to this tea?"

"Nothing, ma'am," Stella replied politely. "It's the same tea you always have."

But you *put three spoonfuls of sugar in it, remember?*

Reading the signs of his lover's mood, Mr Preston smiled one of his confident, amused grins. "What on earth is the matter, Josephine? You seem annoyed."

"It's this ridiculous circus of dressing in black all the time," Mrs Bosworth said, exasperated. "I am thoroughly fed up with playing the part of the grieving widow."

He chuckled. "Take heart, my dear. It's only for a few more months. And then you will be a free woman."

"None too soon, if you ask me. Two years of my life wasted, mourning for that fat pig."

She scoffed at the memory of her late husband. "It's still beyond me why the feeble fool needed to go all the way to Africa, just for those silly butterflies of his."

"Be grateful that he did," Mr Preston sniggered. "If he hadn't died of that tropical fever, he would still be here today." He reached out to touch her hand. "And where would that have left us?"

Deliberately or not, Mrs Bosworth disengaged herself from his touch by reaching for her cup.

"His death was a dreadful nuisance nonetheless," she said. She tried her overly sweet tea again, and winced.

Stella was shocked to hear them talking about the late Mr Bosworth like this. It was true the man hadn't earned much respect from anyone, with his weakness of character and his all-consuming obsession with butterflies. But for Mrs Bosworth and Mr Preston to speak of him as if he had been nothing more than a hindrance – someone who had stood in the way of their adulterous happiness. That was simply too rich, in Stella's opinion.

And to make matters worse, they did so with members of staff in attendance. She was astounded at just how invisible she appeared to be to her masters. They chatted about the most intimate secrets to each other, as if the maid wasn't even there.

I must have become part of the furniture.

"While we are on the topic, Josephine," Mr Preston said casually. "Don't you think it's time you started considering your options?"

"My options?" she replied playfully. "And what would those be, Charles?"

"Well, you could follow the Queen's example. Keep on mourning your late husband and remain a lonely, devoted widow until the end of your days."

His voice was dripping with sarcasm.

"Or?" she asked, dismissing that option outright.

"Or, you could remarry." He leaned back comfortably, staring into her eyes. "You are still young, and there is so much life and energy left in you. Why not share that gift with the right man?"

"Charles, you flatter me. Do you happen to know a suitable candidate?" Mrs Bosworth leaned in closer to him. "One who would appreciate these gifts of mine?"

Stella found it distasteful the way they were playing a coy little piece of theatre. She understood pleasantries, and she even knew about flirting. But this conversation was making her sick to the stomach.

I'd rather scrub pots and pans in the scullery than having to stand here and listen to this tosh.

"As a matter of fact, I do," Mr Preston replied.

"Really?" Mrs Bosworth said, feigning innocence. "Pray tell."

"You know very well who I mean," he grinned. "Myself, of course."

"Charles, darling," she gasped, pretending to be surprised. "Is that a marriage proposal?"

He took her hand in his, while a smouldering intensity took over his penetrating gaze. "We would be perfect together, Josephine. The two of us, we are made for each other."

Eew! Yuck. Stella wished the two of them would save this sort of conversation for the privacy of their bedchamber.

For several heartbeats, Mrs Bosworth revelled in the passion that permeated the air between herself and her suitor. Then, she elegantly slipped her hand out of his tender grip and regained her composure.

"It's too soon," she spoke, making her back regally strong and straight. Her words had the effect of pouring ice-cold water on Mr Preston's fire.

"Too soon? How much longer are you planning to wait?" Her answer clearly had displeased him. "Your late husband has been dead for nearly two years. Time to move on and enjoy life again."

An amused little smile played on Mrs Bosworth's face, and Stella thought that perhaps the mistress was enjoying being in control of the conversation like this.

"I assure you it has nothing to do with any prudishness from my side, dear," she grinned. "But I don't wish to be rushed into any marriage either."

"This wouldn't be just any marriage," he said in a slightly grumpy tone. "You'd be married to *me*."

Now it was her turn to take his hand in hers. "My poor Charles," she soothed. "It sounds like I have hurt your feelings."

"Of course you haven't. Don't talk nonsense," he said as he pulled away his hand, betraying that his feelings – or perhaps his pride rather – had indeed been hurt.

"Oh, good. I like a bit of strength in a man." She smirked, satisfied to have scored this little victory over him. "It's just that I think I would like to enjoy my freedom for a while, before I decide to betroth myself to another man."

"I understand," he said rather sourly. Suddenly, he got up and straightened his clothes. "Don't wait too long to make up your mind though."

His eyes went round the room and settled on Stella briefly.

"Or else," he sneered, "others might decide they like their freedom too."

Stella shifted from one foot to another, growing uncomfortable under his gaze. Charles Preston was the only man Stella knew whose smile was more terrifying than his frown. He had a way of smiling with his lips, while the rest of his face remained emotionless. The sort of smile that sent cold shivers down her spine.

"Charles, darling," Mrs Bosworth said, unimpressed by his demand. "Aren't you being a tad overdramatic? You know I love you."

The darkness lifted from his face, and a radiant yet artificial smile took over. "I am glad we are still clear on that then. Nevertheless," –he leaned over to her, bringing his face close to hers– "I would like to get a final answer from you by summertime."

"And you shall have it," she replied confidently, while presenting him with her cheek, to signal it was time for him to leave.

He kissed her goodbye and went towards the door. "See you next week?"

She nodded. "Same time, please. Ta-ta for now, dear."

After Mr Preston had left, silence fell over the room. Holding her breath for fear of making any noise, Stella wished that she really was invisible. Even though her mistress appeared to have come out of this encounter as the winner, there was no telling which way her mood might swing next.

"Emma?"

Mrs Bosworth's voice had sounded fairly neutral. And Stella thought she even detected an unfamiliar undertone of friendliness. But she was on her guard nonetheless.

"Yes, ma'am?"

"You may take all of this away now," Mrs Bosworth said, casually gesturing at the tea and biscuits.

"Yes, ma'am," she replied, moving in quickly. Her nerves were screaming through her body. *Clear the table and get out*, her mind urged her anxiously.

In the short time it took her to place everything on her large serving tray, her hands started trembling under the strain of the tense moment.

Don't mess this up, Stella.

"Emma?"

She squeezed down hard on the handles of the tray, to steady her hands, bracing herself for what might come next.

"Yes, Mrs Bosworth?"

"Be sure to share this juicy piece of gossip with all the staff, won't you?"

"Ma'am?"

What sort of devious trap was this?

But Mrs Bosworth merely sneered wickedly and said, "Oh, just get out already, you dimwitted girl."

"Yes, ma'am," Stella curtsied. *I'll be delighted to!*

Chapter Twenty-Five

It was past midnight when Stella made her way back from the outdoor privy across the large yard of the country estate. She could just as easily have used the chamber pot up in her room obviously, but it was so hot and stuffy high up under the eaves. So she had decided to go to the servants' toilet outside instead.

The cool summer night air, as well as the many countryside sounds and scents that the breeze brought along from the fields and meadows, had all helped to clear her mind a bit.

She wouldn't have claimed that she was happy, but she was feeling a sense of calm resignation. And that was good enough for her.

Stella's life remained as lonely and isolated as before, but she was beginning to think that maybe this was simply the way of things when you were a maid. And that the friendship she had once known had been nothing but a brief and fleeting moment. Almost like a dream. Perhaps one day, far away in the future, she would actually come to believe that it had been a dream.

Lost deep in thought, she didn't notice the figure standing in the dark and leaning against a wall. When he spoke to her, she gave a start and stopped in her tracks.

"You're up late," the deep voice of Charles Preston said.

Her heart pounding wildly in her throat, Stella had to take a moment to breathe deeply before she answered.

"Yes, sir. Sorry, sir."

In the darkness, she couldn't make out his face. But she knew him well enough by now to imagine him with that typical arrogant smile of his.

He flicked away the cigarette he had been smoking. "Did I startle you?"

"No, sir."

She wanted to continue on her way, but he took a few steps towards her and she felt obliged to stand still.

"Seemed like it though," he said.

"I wasn't expecting to find you here at this late hour, sir."

"Nor I you. But what a pleasant surprise."

He stopped in front of her, and in the light of the full moon she could see his flickering eyes.

This is wrong.

She felt goosebumps appearing on her arms, so she rubbed them with her hands to make them go away.

"I see you're cold, my dear," he said, putting too much friendly concern in his voice.

Dear? He had never addressed her like that before. *And he shouldn't either!* She was a maid after all.

"I'm quite all right, sir," she lied, trying to keep her limbs from shivering.

"That's not what my eyes are telling me," he replied, looking her up and down without any hint of shame.

Stella felt terribly naked. Given that she hadn't planned on bumping into anyone at this hour, she had only thrown a large shawl over her nightgown. Underdressed and with her hair hanging loose, while being eyed up by a man at least twice her age, she couldn't help but blush.

"Now what is that?" he asked in that smooth-talking tone of his. "Is it the freshness of the air that makes your cheeks turn red?" Closing the distance between them, he gently touched her cheek. "Or is that the effect of my presence?"

Stella pulled away. "I'm afraid it's the freshness of the air, sir. And I would quite like to return to my bed because of it."

His gaze was still upon her, as if trying to pry its way underneath her clothes. Instinctively, she wrapped her arms in front of her bosom.

"We don't always get what we like, Stella."

Her jaw dropped. "You know my real name?"

Mr Preston laughed, and she could see his white teeth. She could also smell tobacco and alcohol on his breath.

"Josephine knows your name too, my dear. She just prefers to give you a different one. It's one of those silly power games she loves to play so much, I suppose. I prefer to call you Stella though. It's such a beautiful name."

She flinched when his hand reached out and slowly draped a lock of her hair over her shoulder.

"Don't be afraid, Stella," he said, starting to gently stroke her hair. "I am merely appreciating your beauty. There aren't many men who do, I take it?"

She didn't know how to respond. She wanted to get away from him, but it felt like she stood nailed to the ground, frozen with fear. Something began to feel wrong in her stomach, and she thought she might throw up.

"She said yes, you know," he stated casually while he continued to stroke and admire her hair.

Stella blinked, her nervous mind not understanding what he was talking about.

"Josephine," he clarified. "She has agreed to marry me." He finally stopped stroking her hair and dropped his hand again.

"Congratulations, sir," she replied flatly. Not that she was happy for them, but it seemed like the right thing to say.

He nodded his thanks.

"It's a shame you have to wear a uniform like the rest of the servants," he said. "The good Lord did not make your hair so shiny and your body so attractive to be hidden away underneath those awful, boring clothes."

She let out a short shriek when he suddenly pulled her close and pressed her against himself. Holding her firmly by her arms, he whispered in her ear.

"If it were up to me, you would serve our tea in your birthday suit. So I could better admire the fullness of your beauty."

In an instant, Stella snapped out of her numbness and pushed him away.

"Stop it," she hissed. "It's not right for you to speak to me like that. And you know it... sir!" She put as much defiance in that last word as she could muster.

Turning around, she hurried away from him. But he grabbed her from behind and pulled her to him again.

"Oh, so you think you can tell me what's right and wrong, do you?" he growled, breathing down her neck.

With her arms wound tightly around her waist, he kissed the side of her neck. His stubble prickled her skin. She tried to escape, but he had her in his strong, vice-like grip. And he seemed to enjoy her struggling.

"I'll tell Mrs Bosworth," she whimpered in terror. "She'll be furious to hear–"

Covering her mouth with a single hand, he chuckled, "You need to be quiet, my little darling. You don't want to wake up the whole house, do you?"

He now only had one hand left to restrain her arms, but he was much bigger and stronger than her.

"Don't you know what it would look like," he scoffed, "if they saw you in my arms? Tell Josephine whatever you want. It will only get you fired."

Angry, and desperate to escape, Stella did the only thing she could. She bit his finger.

He cursed and released her mouth. But just as quickly, he spun her around and slapped her in the face.

"You forget your place, my pretty one," he growled as he held her by her arms once more. "I shall be your master soon. Josephine is mine. And so will be this house and every servant in it, as soon as she marries me."

Staring her straight in the eye, he added, "If you think you can refuse me, you are sorely mistaken."

Before she could say anything, he forced his lips on hers and gave her a rough kiss. He tasted rank and sour. Then he shoved her away, seemingly satisfied at having asserted his dominance.

"Go on," he grinned. "Get back inside. You can return to your warm bed now – to dream of the next time we meet. And trust me, it will be somewhere more comfortable and less public."

Stella stumbled away and ran towards the servants' entrance. Behind her, Charles Preston's laughter echoed across the yard.

She hurried up the narrow stairs to her room without looking back, afraid she would see him following her.

Safely back in her bed moments later, she was still quivering. And she knew it wasn't because of the chilly night outside. She had the sudden urge to wash herself, as her entire body felt dirty. Even though he hadn't had his evil way with her – this time – she felt unclean.

Pulling the covers over her head, she squeezed her eyes shut and tried to forget everything that had just happened.

But the fear and panic remained.

Because now she had an even bigger problem on her hands. Mr Preston's advances were a dangerous threat looming over her. How had she got herself into this terrible mess? And more importantly, how could she get out of it?

Pete would know, she thought.

But she still clearly remembered the angry words he had spoken to her that day when she had turned and walked away. *Don't come running back to me*, he had warned her.

Surely though, this was an altogether different matter? This wasn't the housekeeper or Mrs Bosworth making her life difficult. Or the other maids bullying her. This was a man – a man in a position of power and authority over her – wanting to force himself upon her.

If she couldn't confide in Pete about something as serious as that, then who could she turn to? No one!

Oh, why did I have to go outside in the middle of the night? Me and my fanciful ideas!

Getting too hot underneath the covers, she threw them off. Burying her face in her pillow wouldn't solve her problems anyway, she decided.

She took a deep breath, held it for a few heartbeats, and then let it out in a long and soul-cleansing sigh that made her feel more clear-headed.

She had endured hardship and bullying, she reminded herself – first at the workhouse and then at the Bosworths'. And although it wasn't easy, she had coped without the friendship of Pete and Alfie. So she would find a way to live with this new threat as well.

Taking stock of the challenges she had managed to overcome in the past, she started to feel slightly more confident about the future.

After all, with all the trouble that had happened to her so far, things couldn't possibly get much worse, could they?

Chapter Twenty-Six

Alfie wasn't in his room when Stella came to collect the empty tray his morning tea had been served on. Had he finally been let outside again? A little smile crept over her face. She would have loved to have seen him, and perhaps even exchange a quick, wordless glance. But if his mother was beginning to allow him out of his room more, then she was happy for him.

The situation also presented her with an ideal opportunity. She had smuggled Alfie's book along on their annual move to the countryside. Maybe now was the right moment for her to return it after all this time.

She giggled when she imagined the surprised look on Alfie's face when he found it in his room later on. Nobody else would notice one more book lying around, but he would know. And he would know that he was still on her mind.

It was perfect.

Thinking on her feet, she decided to race up to her room, fetch the book from underneath her mattress and carefully place it in his room. Her small attic room was a fair distance away from his room, but if she hurried, she was sure there would be enough time.

It had to work, she told herself. For Alfie's sake as much as for her own.

When she got back to his room with the borrowed book, she was out of breath. She stood there, panting, while scanning the room for the best place to leave the book.

It mustn't be too conspicuous, she thought. *Where would Alfie lay down a book?*

It had to be somewhere his mother would be unlikely to spot it, but where he would eventually still find it.

A stack of drawings on the table caught her eye. What if she hid the book underneath them? As if it were part of the pile.

She went over to the table, holding the book with one arm while she tried to lift up the stack of drawings with her other hand. There were a lot of them and she had to be careful, since she didn't want to risk sending them sliding to the floor.

They were very well done too she couldn't help but notice. Had Alfie made these? She remembered how he had joked once about telling his mother he wanted to take up outdoor painting. Then, according to his cunning plan, he could ask Stella to carry his supplies for him, giving them an excuse to chat as much as they wanted.

She had dismissed his idea as unrealistic of course, but it seemed Alfie had indeed taken up art and drawing. To fight off the boredom of being stuck in his room no doubt.

His favourite subject was horses obviously. But he had been drawing portraits and sketches of people too. Fascinated, she looked at some of his work. She smiled when she spotted a study of Pete's head with his curly hair. Drawn from memory, yet true to life.

But she gave a slight gasp of surprise when she thought she recognised her own features. And not just one but several drawings too. Carefully, she picked up one of her portraits and held it up, to better admire it.

Surely, I don't look that pretty... Do I?

The girl in the drawing was unmistakably her. But he hadn't drawn her like a simple maid. More like the daughter of a wealthy family, with her hair done up and a string of pearls around her neck.

Flattered by his beautiful rendering of her, and daydreaming about this vision of his, she didn't hear the pair of feet coming down the upstairs landing. Suddenly, the door flew open and Stella got the shock of her life when she saw Mrs Bosworth and Alfie, still looking somewhat hot and sweaty from their walk.

She quickly dropped both the drawing and the book on the table, but it was too late. She had been caught.

"What are you doing searching my son's belongings?" Mrs Bosworth demanded to know snootily.

"I wasn't– I mean, I was only–" Stella looked behind her helplessly, begging her mind to come up with a plausible excuse.

The expression on her face tight and menacing, Mrs Bosworth came stomping over to her.

"You were trying to steal from us, weren't you?" she growled. "I saw you holding that book."

"No, ma'am. Honestly, I wasn't," Stella said, her voice shaky and frightened – which, she realised, probably wasn't helping her mistress' perception.

"You thief!" Mrs Bosworth shrieked, as she grabbed Stella by the arm and squeezed down hard on it. "I'll show you what we do to filthy little thieves in this house."

"Please, ma'am," Stella squeaked. "You're hurting me."

"You will be in much more pain than this when I'm through with you, you miserable workhouse rat."

Mrs Bosworth let go of Stella's arm, but then grabbed her by the hair instead and started dragging her towards the door.

Hot flashes of vicious pain shot through Stella's skull, instantly driving tears to her eyes. She yelped, and feared Mrs Bosworth would rip out her hair.

"Mother, stop!" Alfie yelled in a panic. "She wasn't stealing the book."

Mrs Bosworth stopped, but held onto Stella's hair.

"Of course she was. You saw her. Don't be such a naive fool, Alfie."

"No, she wasn't."

Had his voice just sounded slightly more confident and a bit defiant even?

"She couldn't be stealing the book," he said. "Because I lent it to her."

Mrs Bosworth let go of Stella's hair.

"You what?!" she asked her son, incredulously.

"I gave it to her a while ago, so she could read it." He was much calmer now, and he kept his shoulders straight. "Stella was merely returning the book."

There was a stunned silence, as Mrs Bosworth stood staring at her son.

"So there's no need for you to treat her so harshly," Alfie continued, emboldened by his mother's speechless reaction.

Mrs Bosworth narrowed her eyes however, and said through gritted teeth, "Don't tell me what to do, you impudent boy."

Her hand lashed out and landed hard across Alfie's face. Stella shrieked as she saw his head turn to the side under the force of his mother's slap.

"Mrs Bosworth, please," she begged.

Furiously, the mistress spun round to her and slapped her in the face as well.

"And no one tells me how I should treat my staff!"

Stella and Alfie both stood holding a hand to their painful faces. Their hopes had been dashed, and their brief moment of defiance was over.

"I shall deal with you later," Mrs Bosworth said, pointing a finger at her son. "I will teach you to fraternise with the staff like that. Nothing good can come of a man who doesn't learn to disregard the maid."

Stella wisely decided not to mention her recent nighttime encounter with Mr Preston.

"And as for you," Mrs Bosworth told her, "I have just the punishment for you."

Grabbing Stella by the arm, she marched her out of the room and down the stairs.

"Mother, what are you going to do to her?" Alfie asked, following them on their heels.

"Go back to your room," his mother barked.

"I demand to know what you intend to do with Stella."

Mrs Bosworth stopped and shot an angry look at her son. "You demand? I can see I have been too lenient with you. That will have to change."

Ignoring him completely, she continued dragging Stella behind her.

"Mrs Burch!" Mrs Bosworth bellowed once they got downstairs. Not waiting for a reply, she made her way to the kitchens, still clinging on to Stella who had no choice but to stumble along.

Would she be fired now, Stella wondered? And did that mean she would be left stranded here in the countryside?

The startled housekeeper appeared in the kitchen doorway just as Mrs Bosworth was about to barge through that same door.

"Ah, Mrs Burch," the mistress spoke sternly. "This miserable excuse for a maid is to be confined to scullery duties."

"I see," Mrs Burch replied, wringing her hands awkwardly. "And for how long, Mrs Bosworth?"

"Indefinitely."

"Oh dear. I'm so sorry to hear that, Mrs Bosworth. She's usually quite a decent maid. One of the best we've had in a long time in fact."

Stella was surprised to hear such high praise coming from the housekeeper.

"I don't care," Mrs Bosworth replied irritably. "You will simply have to find another one. Because as soon as we return to London, I'm sending this one back to the workhouse. Where she belongs."

"Mother, no!" Alfie gasped from behind her back.

"Stay out of this, Alfred. And don't cause a scene. Especially not in front of the staff."

Stella could see Cook and several more servants looking on in the background. Margaret and Esther were among them too.

"As you wish, ma'am," Mrs Burch relented. "I suppose I shall have her swap places with the current scullery maid for now."

"Do with her as you please, Mrs Burch. As long as you keep her out of my sight, and as far away from my son as possible."

Mrs Bosworth shoved Stella in the direction of the kitchen. "Enjoy your pots and pans, you little wretch," she hissed.

Glancing over her shoulder one final time, Stella saw Alfie looking sadly at her. *I'm sorry*, he mouthed silently.

She nodded and entered the kitchen. Most of the servants present regarded her with shock. But when she passed Margaret and Esther, she could clearly see the contempt and glee in their eyes.

Hesitating on the doorstep that led into the damp scullery, she heard the two maids sniggering behind her back.

"Enjoy your pots and pans," they giggled viciously.

Stella stepped inside the scullery, and vowed not to cry, so they wouldn't see her tears.

Unfortunately, she failed.

Chapter Twenty-Seven

Aside from Alfie's life as a virtual prisoner in his own home, her rupture with Pete, as well as Mr Preston's unwelcome advances, being a scullery maid hadn't exactly made Stella's life any easier. It was demanding work, scouring and scrubbing greasy pots and pans and any other kitchen utensils that needed cleaning.

And then there was the seemingly never-ending stream of delicate plates, saucers and teacups, not to mention the fine silverware that required special attention. Because heaven forbid if she broke or scratched anything! She had no idea about the precise value of the tableware, but it looked expensive. And she was fairly sure a week's worth of her wages would barely cover the price of a single one of those pretty china plates.

But there was always so much to wash up, she could ill afford to work slowly. So she scrubbed her days away, until her arms were sore and the skin on her hands turned raw in the lukewarm water.

And when all the washing up was finally done, Cook or Mrs Burch would usually find other chores and tasks for her, like scrubbing the dirty kitchen floor or stirring the large tub of smelly, soapy water containing the weekly wash of clothes and bed sheets. Basically, anything the other servants turned up their noses at.

But Stella didn't complain. The hard work kept her mind busy, which otherwise would have been sick with feelings of concern for Alfie – or plagued with guilt and anger about her problems with Pete.

Mr Preston was a different issue however. She tried to banish any thoughts of him to the furthest corners of her mind. But always she sensed the memory of that frightful incident lurking in the darkness, just like he had been doing that night. Her strategy was to avoid him completely. And in that respect, her demotion to lowly scullery maid was a stroke of good luck. Because Mr Preston had no chance or reason to come into the scullery. Fate could be both weirdly cruel and merciful like that.

Whenever she was haunted by visions of his wickedly grinning face, and what he had tried to do with her, she would angrily scrub and clean with so much vigour until she was out of breath and the memory went away.

No, Stella mused, it wasn't the work that bothered her. It was the other people in the household. And Margaret and Esther were decidedly the worst. The eldest maid Lily had left a few months earlier to get married, but Margaret was proving to be a worthy successor as chief tormentor and head bully. Stella hadn't expected it any different.

She was far more disappointed in Esther though. The former scullery maid revelled in her newly elevated status, and took to taunting Stella with a sadistic passion. Together, Margaret and Esther didn't miss any opportunity to make her feel the change in the pecking order.

Most of the other servants paid her no attention. As the scullery maid, she was like a ghost to them. Probably even less, for at least a ghost was considered scary. Stella however was a harmless shadow on the wall, as much a part of the kitchen furnishings as the oven or the sink.

The only two faces who never failed to grin and snigger at her with glee were those of Margaret and Esther. They would laugh and whisper in each other's ear.

"Doesn't she look a bit tired to you today?" Esther asked Margaret.

"Maybe the poor thing doesn't get enough sleep," the other one replied snarkily.

"Strange. You'd think she would be getting more sleep now that she can't secretly visit her precious little prince any longer."

Stella ignored their cackling. In the beginning, she had tried to hit back at them with witty remarks, but that only made matters worse. So she chose to keep silent. Instead, she glared at them darkly from a safe distance.

"What's the matter, princess?" Esther said in Stella's direction. "Lost your tongue from reading stolen books?"

"Or maybe it's all that carbolic soap and soda she's exposed to!"

Let them laugh and have their cruel fun, Stella thought. *It's what simple people do.*

Engaging with them and talking back only fuelled their hatred. If she refused to be angered by their words, she showed herself to be stronger and better than them.

And they didn't like that.

"Here, watch this," she heard Esther whispering to Margaret as she carried a tray of clean plates to the large kitchen cupboard.

Guessing the meaning of the words too late, Stella didn't see Esther suddenly sticking out her leg, and tripped over it.

Her tray hit the floor with a clatter, smashing some of the plates to pieces. It was a loud clangour, and because she tried to protect the plates as she fell, she herself hit the ground hard.

As she lay on the cold kitchen floor, simultaneously shocked and furious, she was dying to make Esther feel the palm of her hand. A hot wave of anger and embarrassment flowed through her body, and she was about to pick herself up, when a strong hand pulled her to her feet.

She looked up, and found herself staring straight into the eyes of Pete. His face was cool and emotionless.

The surprise of seeing him drowned out Esther and Margaret's mocking laughter in the background. Stella was speechless. Pete had intervened and come to her aid?!

Before she regained her senses and got a chance to thank him however, he looked away and turned around to the sneering maids.

"You two!" he said, in a tone that put an immediate end to their laughter. "Do you think this is funny? Breaking things? Perhaps you won't find it so funny anymore when Mrs Burch makes you pay for the damage from your wages."

Esther's eyes widened. "We didn't break anything. She did."

"I saw you trip her up deliberately! So it's you who'll take the blame for this."

Esther opened her mouth to protest, but Pete cut her off. "And you can begin by brushing up the pieces."

Then he turned to Margaret. "You. Go to Mrs Burch straight away and tell her Esther broke..." –he scanned the floor to assess the damage– "three plates."

The two maids hesitated briefly.

"Now!" Pete barked with a rumbling voice.

Startled into action, Esther hurried to fetch the dustpan and brush, while Margaret went to look for Mrs Burch, visibly relieved to get away from Pete's anger.

Avoiding any eye contact with Stella, he supervised Esther as she cleaned up all the broken pieces and every little shard.

Stella stood by and watched, silently in awe of his strong and firm handling of the situation. She wished she too could have a presence and authority as calm and powerful as his.

When Esther was finished, she turned up her nose and made off offendedly, her tiny footsteps resounding on the walls and ceiling of the otherwise eerily quiet kitchen.

After a few heartbeats, Stella gathered up her courage and said, softly, "Thank you." She wanted to reach out to him, and to be closer to him. But she kept her distance. Her heart was still beating wildly, albeit for different reasons now.

Pete finally turned his head towards her. He seemed less confident than he had been with the bullying maids. She thought he might say something to her, but instead, he only gave her a short, awkward smile.

Then he took one final quick look round the kitchen. "Let me know if they give Mrs Burch a different story than what I told them to say."

"I will. Pete–"

"I have to go," he said, and went outside again.

Stella stared after him through the open door until he was gone, out of sight. Out of reach.

She lowered herself onto the wooden bench at the table, and put her hand over her heart to calm its frantic beating.

Pete had defended her.

Despite the awfulness of the incident, she couldn't help but smile. Because clearly, he still cared about her.

Chapter Twenty-Eight

Timidly, Stella entered the breakfast room to clear the table. That wasn't the task of the scullery maid normally, but Cook had sent her anyway.

"Those people would draw their breakfast out until midday if I let them," the plump mistress of the kitchen had scoffed. "But I need those plates and cutlery back so you can scrub and clean them in time. I've got better things to do than to sit around waiting for them."

Bracing herself for Mrs Bosworth's reaction, Stella wheeled her little serving trolley inside, hoping against hope that nobody would take notice of her.

"What are *you* doing here?" the familiar sneering voice asked.

Here we go.

"Cook instructed me to come and clear the breakfast table, ma'am."

"And I thought I had instructed Mrs Burch to keep you out of our sights."

"Terribly sorry, ma'am," Stella said, keeping her eyes to the ground. "But I believe the other maids are busy changing the beds at the moment, and there was only me left."

"Hang on," Mr Preston interrupted the argument. He looked at his fiancée and asked, "What did you do?"

"I asked the housekeeper to confine this girl to the scullery from now on."

"What for?" he chuckled. "Has she been naughty?"

He eyed Stella with a ravenous, cheeky look.

"Must everything be a jolly jape to you, Charles?" Mrs Bosworth sighed. "I caught her stealing."

"No, you didn't," Alfie spoke up. "She wasn't stealing!"

"Be silent, Alfie," his mother hissed.

Mr Preston seemed to enjoy the exchange.

"So is this why that daft, dimwitted girl has been serving us lately?" he asked. "What's her name? Esther? The one with the funny teeth?"

Tilting his head, he did a crude impersonation of someone with a huge overbite while crossing his eyes, and then laughed at his own joke.

Mrs Bosworth rolled her eyes. "I shall not have you questioning my decisions about how to manage the staff, Charles."

"I'm not questioning anything, my darling. I merely wish to point out to you that good staff is increasingly hard to find these days. It would be a shame to lose a capable and skilled hand."

His twinkling eyes were piercing Stella, who could guess what his definition of 'capable' was.

"Let her stay and do her job," he said nonchalantly. With a casual wave of the hand, he gestured at their table to her. "Go on, girl. Attend to your duties."

Unsure about what to do and who was in charge here, she looked at Mrs Bosworth.

"You heard Mr Preston," her mistress snapped. "Clear this table and then get out."

"Yes, ma'am."

"But not so much as a peep from you."

Trained to always reply to her masters, Stella just about managed to swallow the 'No, ma'am' that was on the tip of her tongue, and simply nodded instead.

She decided to clear Alfie's things first. With her back to his mother, she dared to venture a glance and a quick smile at him. When he had checked that his mother wasn't looking, he smiled back.

"Anyway," Mr Preston announced, "I thought Alfie and I might go for a long ride through the countryside today. We've had nothing but rain for the past week, but now finally, the weather is simply begging us to take the horses out."

"I am not convinced that is such a good idea, Charles," Mrs Bosworth pouted. "Alfie is not to leave his room during the day. As punishment for speaking up against me."

"I understand that. But at the same time, my darling, the boy needs some proper physical exertion every now and then. Or he will end up becoming a weak, effeminate slug."

Stella caught Alfie casting an angry glare at his mother's fiancé.

"Honestly, Charles," Mrs Bosworth said, frowning and increasingly irritated. "I am surprised you should have such a short memory.

You and I both agreed on the correct way to raise Alfie."

Tightening her lips and looking him straight in the eye, she added, "You know exactly what I'm talking about."

She delicately dabbed at her mouth with her napkin and seemed to regain her composure. "Alfred needs to focus on his studies, even in the summertime."

"Tosh and poppycock," Mr Preston replied, dismissing her remark with a wave of his hand. "One ride isn't going to hurt him. Will it, lad?"

Eager to know how this battle of wills would end, Stella deliberately went about her task of clearing the table as slow as she could.

"Fine then," Mrs Bosworth relented, albeit visibly displeased. "What about we take the carriage instead though? It's more relaxing and not as taxing."

"I was thinking more of taking Alfie out by myself. Just me and him. Two men doing manly things."

Mrs Bosworth's vexed pout returned. "Ah," she replied drily, "I see."

"I am glad you see things my way, darling," he said, sounding rather smug. "I knew you would agree. It's why I've already asked the stable boy to prepare the horses."

"How conveniently proactive and forward-looking of you." The sarcasm was thick and palatable beneath Mrs Bosworth's words.

"It's what we men do, my darling. We take action. Don't we, Alfie?"

Alfie nodded. He seemed just as uncertain and ambiguous about this situation as Stella. She was happy for him that he would get a chance to go outside for a ride – something he used to enjoy. But he would be under the control of Mr Preston the entire time. Which was bound to take the fun out of it.

"Speak up, son!" Mr Preston raised his voice, not satisfied with Alfie's meek response.

"Yes, sir," the boy muttered.

"Dear, oh dear. I can see I will have my work cut out with you."

"And what work would that be?" Mrs Bosworth asked. Stella felt it sounded like her mistress wasn't happy with the direction the conversation was taking.

"The work of helping you to raise the boy of course, Josephine."

Laughing, Mr Preston got up and went over to Alfie. As he walked past Stella, he brushed his shoulder across her back. He made it look like he was merely passing by, but she was sure it was a deliberate move.

"I have been coping rather well on my own, thank you," Mrs Bosworth said.

"Of course you have, my darling. You have made him the boy he is today. But now," – standing behind him, Mr Preston placed his hands firmly on Alfie's shoulders– "the time has come to turn him into a man."

Mrs Bosworth raised a skeptical eyebrow. "A man, you say?"

"Indeed," Mr Preston replied confidently. "Alfie needs to be hardened, lose these round cheeks and this puffy angel face of his." Reaching over from behind, he squeezed one of Alfie's cheeks and gave it a little shake.

"Maybe he should grow a beard and a moustache as well. The ladies love that sort of thing." Curling up one side of his own carefully groomed moustache, he gave a hearty laugh.

"Don't worry though, lad. You will learn from the best."

"I am sure that he will," Mrs Bosworth said, clearly not amused by his banter.

Annoyingly full of himself, Mr Preston returned to his seat, kissing his fiancée on the cheek before he sat down again.

"What if I don't want to become a man?" Alfie said quietly. "Not your type of man anyway."

The hush that fell over the room was so intense, Stella froze, the empty teacup in her hand hovering in mid-air.

"I have never heard anything more foolish in my life," Mr Preston scoffed. Turning to his fiancée, he said, "See what you did to him, Josephine? This is unbelievable."

Mrs Bosworth's eyes were cold and deadly as she stared at him. But she didn't say a word, and Stella understood a silence like that was even more dangerous than any word her mistress could have spoken in reply.

Mr Preston seemed unaware of his fiancée's shifting mood however, and pressed on unabated. "You were right about Alfie being disrespectful. So we will correct that straight away."

"How?" Mrs Bosworth's eyes were narrow slits of mistrust and suspicion.

"Stella," Mr Preston said calmly, "go over to Alfie and slap him for me."

The teacup made a loud clattering noise when she dropped it onto a stack of dishes.

For once, she and Mrs Bosworth shared the same sentiment. "She will do no such thing," the mistress bristled. "The maid slapping my son, it's unheard of! Have you lost your senses, Charles?"

"Not at all, my dear. This is simply part and parcel of the type of education that you and I had agreed was right for the boy. Remember?"

"I don't remember agreeing to letting the maid hit my son! It's unseemly, it's degrading, and it's humiliating."

Mrs Bosworth looked like she was ready to slap her fiancé. But he merely raised his hand in defence, and grinned sinisterly, "All the more reason why this punishment must be meted out to him by her."

Even though Stella knew Mr Preston was a vile and despicable man, she hadn't thought it possible he would sink this low. But he just had. She hoped dearly that Mrs Bosworth wouldn't agree to this travesty.

The mistress remained silent for a moment, then swallowed and said, in a weak voice, "I suppose if you put it like that."

Stella couldn't believe her ears! She turned to Alfie, and he looked equally shocked.

"You heard your mistress," Mr Preston said. "Slap that impertinent boy."

Stella looked over at Mrs Bosworth in disbelief. She wanted a word of confirmation, or a simple nod of the head. But her mistress showed no sign of her usual confident arrogance. Instead, Mrs Bosworth averted her eyes and stared at the ground in shame.

Stella slowly stepped towards Alfie, who stood up from his chair to face his punishment.

"And make sure it's hard enough," Mr Preston commanded. "Or I shall make you slap him again until I am satisfied."

Her hands trembling with fear and revulsion at what she was about to do, Stella swallowed hard.

"I'm so sorry," she whispered almost inaudibly.

"It's okay," he replied.

You're my friend, she thought his brave face was telling her.

You're more of a man than he is, she replied in her mind.

Chapter Twenty-Nine

When Stella came into the kitchen with her trolley full of plates, cups and cutlery, her hand was still glowing uncomfortably from the hard slap across the face she had been forced to give Alfie. The emotional hurt was far greater than any physical pain however, and she felt sick to the stomach.

She was already halfway across the kitchen and pushing the trolley towards the scullery, when she noticed Pete's father sitting at a corner of the large table. The senior coachman was quietly eating a late breakfast.

"Oh, good morning, Mr Draper. My apologies, I hadn't seen you there."

"Don't mind me, lass," the grizzled man answered with a friendly smile. "I was up all night attending to a horse that had a bad case of bowel pains. Cook kindly fixed me some breakfast just now."

"I'm sorry to hear that, sir. Is the horse any better this morning?" She knew she had work to do, but it was so wonderful to have a normal conversation with someone nice for a change.

"The horse is fine now, bless the poor beast. Colic can be a dangerous thing for horses, you know?"

"Really?"

He nodded. "Can even kill them."

Glancing around at the deserted kitchen, he gestured at the seat in front of him. "Why don't you sit down and keep an old man company while he has his breakfast?"

His invitation came with such a warm and genuine smile, that she couldn't resist. Clearly, he enjoyed a friendly chat just as much as she did.

"I didn't know that," she said. "About colic being potentially deadly."

"It's why I stayed up all night. To keep an eye on the poor animal, and walk around with it. Makes the bowels move and settle."

"You are so good with horses, Mr Draper," she said admiringly. "I can see where Pete gets his love of horses from."

She had surprised herself by blurting out Pete's name like that in her excitement. She saw his father giving her an examining, thoughtful look.

"And how have you been, Mr Draper?" she quickly enquired, hoping her attempt to steer the subject away from Pete wasn't too obvious.

"Very well thanks. Busy as always, I suppose." He spooned some more food into his mouth and chewed slowly. "But what about you, dear? I haven't seen you around the stables much lately."

So much for keeping that topic off the table.

As if he could read her mind, he smiled and said, "I seem to remember you visiting Pete quite regularly at the stables at one point."

He dismissed her look of surprise and apprehension with a lazy flourish of his spoon. "Don't worry, I never minded. But it's been a while, hasn't it?"

She stared at the table, trying to keep the painful memories at bay.

"Yes," she sighed. "It has been a while."

"What happened? You were such good friends."

She hesitated. Mr Draper seemed like a nice man, but if he found out the details of why and how she had fallen out with Pete – and over whom – he might be less understanding.

"It wasn't something Pete did, was it?" His voice was full of concern, incorrectly guessing at the reason for her awkward silence. "I've tried to raise him to respect girls, but if he–"

"No, no, Mr Draper. It wasn't anything like that."

He was visibly relieved, making her feel even more obliged to provide the sweet old man with some sort of explanation.

"We had a fight – a difference of opinion, you might call it. And I'm afraid we haven't talked since."

"Must have been some argument then, for the two of you not to talk to each other for that long."

She nodded. "What's so stupid about it is I barely remember the words that were spoken. I only remember what we were arguing about. And that we both hurt each other's feelings."

"Yes, fights are silly like that, aren't they? I'm sorry to hear this, Stella. If Pete had told me anything about it, I would've given him a piece of my mind. Friends should be able to make up after an argument."

"That's sweet of you to say, Mr Draper."

"Mind you, that headstrong lad of mine hardly ever tells me anything."

"Oh? I was rather under the impression the two of you enjoyed a good relationship." She remembered Pete telling her about his mother who died when he was young, and the story of his uncle leaving for Germany to avoid a scandal – both incidents that led his father to become very caring and protective of him.

"We do, I suppose, in a way," Mr Draper said. "But men don't talk about these things very often. I love him more than I love my own life. And I know he loves me. But we could never say that to each other of course."

"Of course."

How sad, she thought. But she also knew how hard it sometimes was to say those words out loud to each other.

"We were really good friends," she said, the sadness in her voice apparent. "Pete and I could talk about anything to each other. I feel so lonely without him. Especially when so many people seem to enjoy bullying me. Between the other maids and Mrs Bosworth, I don't know what to do."

"Then go to Pete and talk to him."

He made it sound so simple. And perhaps it was.

But she and Pete had fought over something fundamentally important. They had argued about friendship and loyalty, and whether Alfie was worth helping, even if it could land them in serious trouble.

Her opinion hadn't changed. She wouldn't apologise for wanting to be a true friend to Alfie.

On the other hand...

The whole situation weighed on her like a heavy boulder on her back, and the sensation of being crushed grew stronger every day. She didn't know how much longer she would be able to carry that burden. If the only way to get her dearest friend and companion back was by swallowing her pride, then wasn't that worth the brief sting?

Mr Draper studied her face, and smiled. "Listen," he said, "I'm no expert, but I know Pete is a good lad. He's just as young and insecure as you are. And he's probably afraid of being hurt, which is why he's keeping his distance."

"So I've noticed," Stella murmured.

"But he wouldn't be doing that if he didn't care for you. So either the two of you continue to avoid each other. Or..."

He shrugged, and Stella knew what his advice was going to be.

"Or we forget about the argument and start talking to each other again," she said. "But that would feel like giving in somehow. Like admitting I was wrong. Our fight was about something that is really important to me."

"I can imagine. Making up is hard, I know. But by now Pete surely has had enough time to think about it as well. Maybe he has even come to agree with you a bit more. Maybe he is too proud to tell you, just like you are. All he needs is a little push. And then everything will fall into place again."

"But what if it doesn't? What if I end up making things worse?"

"How much worse can it get if the two of you aren't even talking?" Mr Draper chuckled. "If it doesn't work out, then at least you'll have tried and you can move on. Instead of wasting precious time and energy thinking about what could have been."

She thought about that for a while.

"You're right," she said. "I'll talk to him."

"Good lass. When?"

She bit her lip. "After I'm done scrubbing in the scullery?"

"How about right now?" Mr Draper winked. "Those pots and pans can wait."

"Thank you, Mr Draper," she said, leaping to her feet, feeling so much lighter already. "For everything."

The smile on his face wrinkled the skin around his eyes, but it didn't make him look older.

"You're welcome," he replied. "Now go."

Chapter Thirty

Without any further hesitation, Stella left her trolley where she had put it – in the middle of the kitchen. Mr Draper was right. Talking to Pete was more important than dirty dishes. And making amends with him was more important than anything else she could think of right now.

If Cook or Mrs Burch found out she had abandoned the scullery like this, there would probably be hell to pay. But she didn't care in the slightest. Pete, and their friendship, was all that mattered.

Leaving Mr Draper to finish his breakfast, she dashed out of the kitchen and ran across the big yard to the stables.

The closer she got to the big stable doors, the more nervously hopeful she became. It was a good feeling. She and Pete would talk, and things would be better again. Like they were before. How silly she had been, she thought, to not have done this sooner.

I guess sometimes our foolish pride just gets in the way of what our heart knows is best.

The doors to the stables were open, and she rushed through them, fully expecting to see Pete's surprised face there. Would he smile at her straight away, equally happy to see her?

But there was no Pete.

In fact, it appeared there wasn't anyone around in the stables. Standing in the middle of the wide central corridor, she caught her breath and then called out his name.

The only reply she got came from Atlantis. Alfie's horse stood tied outside his stable box, saddled up and ready for his ride with his human master. Next to him was another horse, which Stella assumed was meant for Mr Preston.

"Hey boy," she greeted him as she walked over to the horses. "Are you two waiting for Alfie and Mr Preston?"

Atlantis recognised her and was happy to let her stroke his mane.

"Have you seen Pete, Atlantis?" She looked around the stables, but there was no sign of anyone. "And why am I asking you?" she giggled.

"It's not as if you'd be able to answer my question."

She patted his neck and sighed. "I guess I'll have to try and come back later. Let's hope I get the chance. Because if Cook or Mrs Burch find out I left the kitchen to come out here, I'm sure to be punished with extra chores. Will you tell Pete I said hello?"

Atlantis gave her a friendly little shove with his head.

"I like you too," she smiled. "You enjoy your ride with Alfie, okay?"

Reluctantly, she started walking back. But as she glanced through one of the stable windows, her heart suddenly froze.

Mr Preston was coming towards the stables!

A cold fear gripped her. Was he merely coming over to collect the horses for their ride? Or had he spotted her and was he following her around?

He mustn't find me here, her head screamed. Because even if it was purely by coincidence, if he bumped into her in the deserted stables, he was sure to try something wicked and depraved again.

And this time, she might not be so lucky to escape him.

Panicking, she looked about her like a frightened rabbit searching for the nearest hole to disappear in. There was only one way in or out of the stables. So she needed to hide somewhere, and quickly too. But where?

The hay loft! That was her best chance.

She raced up the short and steep flight of narrow wooden stairs. The hay loft overlooked the central corridor and one side of the stable boxes. So she dove into a big pile of hay, hoping she would be hidden from view that way.

She'd worry about her clothes later. Staying out of Mr Preston's vile hands was more important than keeping her maid's uniform clean.

Her fearful heart was beating so wildly in her chest, and she was breathing so fast, that she was afraid the sounds would give her presence away.

Mr Preston was whistling a simple tune when he entered the stables. "Morning," he called out to nobody in particular. "Anyone about?"

He remained silent for a moment, and then she heard his boots walking further down the corridor, slowly. His footsteps sounded hollow and ominous on the hard floor.

Would he be coming up to the loft? Or was he only checking up on the horses? The suspense was killing her.

Gingerly, she crawled a bit closer to the edge of the open hay loft. From this position, she could just about see him while still being hidden from view. Or so she hoped.

Mr Preston walked over to the saddled horses.

"Ready and waiting for our ride, eh?" he said. "Listen, old boy. I want you to do me a favour." He patted Atlantis, who turned his head round at him, seemingly suspicious of this new visitor.

"Don't worry. I'm not going to hurt you." He chuckled. "It's that young master of yours I intend to harm. A great deal."

Stella heard Atlantis chomp down on something.

"Yes, you like a good carrot, don't you?" Mr Preston said. "And I've got another one for you, if you promise to stand still for me. There's something I need to do, you see. But you can't tell anyone, you hear, old boy?"

What was he up to? Why did he need to be this secretive? And what was that talk about harming Alfie?

She had to know. So she tried to get as close to the edge of the hay loft platform as she dared, to get a better view.

Spying on him from above, she saw Mr Preston taking out a small object from his pocket. When he flicked it open, there was a brief flash of sunshine reflecting on steel.

Stella nearly screamed, so she covered her mouth with both her hands. Mr Preston was holding a small hunting knife! What on earth was he intending to do with that?

There was a sense of danger in the air. And she knew she wasn't imagining it, because Atlantis felt it too. Alfie's horse made a concerned nickering sound.

"Don't worry, old boy," Mr Preston spoke soothingly. His voice was calm, but something about it unsettled her, like everything about Josephine Bosworth's future husband.

He was standing right next to Atlantis, and he seemed to be working on something that caused him some strain and effort.

"Just need to cut through part of your saddle straps," he groaned. "Not all of it, because that would be too obvious. Just enough for them to snap when we're out riding, so that little fool of yours falls off your back."

Stella gasped. He wanted Alfie to have an accident! This truly was a vile and vicious man.

"Oh, don't look at me like that, old boy," he chuckled. "No one will blame you. It'll be an accident, see? There. That should do it."

He stepped back to admire his dirty work and to check if his sabotage wasn't too visible.

"Yes," he nodded. "A very unfortunate and very fatal accident."

Fatal? He didn't just want to hurt Alfie... He wanted him dead!

Shocked, and unable to help herself, Stella inhaled sharply. Dust from the loose hay she was hiding in entered her nose. She felt it tickling her nostrils and cursed inwardly when she sensed an unstoppable sneeze coming on.

She tried to hold it back... but failed.

"*Tchoo!*"

Below her, Charles Preston froze. "Who's there?" his alarmed voice asked urgently.

Stella buried her face in the hay. She didn't dare crawl back deeper into the pile, for fear of betraying herself even more.

"Show yourself," Mr Preston commanded. "Whoever you are. I won't hurt you."

Like hell you won't.

He would come up to the loft to have a look, and then he was sure to find her. She was certain of it. And he had a knife, she remembered all too well!

Maybe if she kept perfectly still?

Then, as she thought she heard him moving towards the narrow stairs up to the loft, her plight became even more precarious.

A black cat dropped down from a wooden beam above her and startled her. Luckily, she didn't scream or make any more noise. But the silly animal began to playfully rub itself against Stella's face, blissfully unaware of her perilous situation.

Go away, she prayed silently. *Shoo!*

In desperation, and with nothing else to lose, she quickly gave the cat a forceful shove. The animal rolled to the edge of the loft, where it quickly recovered and stood up on its four paws again.

Sorry, kitty!

Deeply insulted, the cat hissed and spat at her, and then strutted defiantly along the edge of the open platform.

"Oh," Mr Preston sighed with relief. "Was that you making those feisty noises up there?"

As if to answer his question, the cat meowed at him, perhaps hoping this man would be nicer than that girl who had just been so rude.

"Gave me an awful fright you did. Bloody cats. Anyone else up there with you?"

Once more, Stella's heart skipped a beat. Was he still intent on having a closer look in the hay loft?

She was saved however by the sound of laughter approaching from outside. She recognised the voice of Tommy and one of the younger lads.

Deciding it was safer to withdraw, Mr Preston left the stables, while putting on his usual air of casual superiority. He completely ignored the stable boys as they doffed their caps and greeted him respectfully.

That was close! Stella let out the long breath she had been holding.

But then, after a wave of relief had washed over her, his words came back to her: he was planning to get Alfie killed during their horse ride.

She jumped to her feet.

There was no time to lose.

Chapter Thirty-One

Stella bounded down the creaky old steps of the narrow hay loft stairs. Through one of the windows, she watched Mr Preston go back inside the main house. That evil villain was going to murder, Alfie! She had to find Pete. But if he wasn't in the stables, then where could he be?

Think, Stella. Think!

"Were you up there as well?" Tommy asked, gazing stupidly at her with his mouth open.

'As well'?

He pointed with his thumb over this shoulder. "We just saw Mr Preston leave the stables, looking a bit dodgy." He grinned, knowingly. "Guess now we understand why. Wait until I tell Pete."

He elbowed the other boy, and they both sneered and chuckled like idiots.

Oh, no! They're assuming I was up there with Mr Preston.

She briefly considered telling him what she had just witnessed and overheard. But she knew he would never believe her. Mr Preston wanting to murder his fiancée's son? Tommy would think she was making up a fanciful story as a poor and unconvincing excuse to explain her presence. She could hardly believe it herself. And yet she had personally heard and witnessed what Mr Preston was up to.

"Stellaaa!" Cook's angry voice sounded from the door to the kitchens. "Where are you? And why aren't you in this kitchen?"

"Uh oh," Tommy sneered. "More trouble, princess. You'd better hurry back. Don't worry though. I'm sure the new master will put in a good word for his plaything with Mrs Burch."

The other boy sniggered, and Tommy winked as he gave him another playful shove with his elbow and pointed at Stella.

"Keep your eyes on this one, lad," he said. "She's got her sights set high, I tell you. Carrying on with both the young master and our soon-to-be older master of the house."

This was going to get nasty she knew. If Tommy started circulating a juicy story claiming she had been rolling in the hay with Charles Preston...

But she couldn't worry about what the rumours would do to her reputation, or even to her position.

Alfie's life was in grave danger.

Pushing past the laughing and leering boys, she marched back to the kitchen. She needed to find Pete, urgently, but she had no other choice than to face up to Cook first.

"Where have you been?" Cook demanded to know.

"I was—"

"And why did you abandon your duties, leaving this trolley in the middle of the kitchen like that?"

"Mr Draper told me I—"

"Don't you dare implicate that sweet man in your mischief!"

"But I was—"

"Loitering about with that lad from the stables again, I bet. Or is it one of the other stable boys that's taken your fancy?"

"I didn't even—"

"Oh, stop talking already."

If the circumstances hadn't been so dire, Stella would have laughed at this ridiculous exchange. She hadn't got a single meaningful word in. Still, if that meant she didn't need to explain herself, she decided she could live with it.

"Take that trolley and get back to work in your scullery," Cook grumbled, settling the affair. "Those pots and pans won't clean themselves, you know."

Even as Stella began washing dirty dishes and scrubbing grubby pans, the panic about Mr Preston's hideous plan didn't let go of her. She simply had to stop him! But how?

I need help, that's what.

She needed to talk to Pete. He was the only one likely to believe her. Telling anyone else would be a useless waste of time. She could imagine the look on the faces of Cook or Mrs Burch if she tried telling them what she had overheard in the stables.

Smack me around the ears is what they would do.

No, Pete was her only hope. But she needed to find him first. Maybe he was out in one of the estate's pastures, tending to the grazing horses there? Or maybe he had since returned to the stables. Perhaps she should attempt to sneak outside again, to go and have another look?

Tentatively, she glanced through the scullery door into the main kitchen. Her shoulders dropped when she saw Cook walking around in there, busily preparing food while muttering to herself. Even if Stella made a dash for it, the mistress of the kitchen would still come after her. And the prospect of being chased by a furious cook waving a big ladle, or worse, didn't quite appeal to her.

An hour later, Stella hadn't got any further with her intention to save Alfie. Her despair had only grown, even as her stack of washing-up dwindled.

Where would Alfie and Mr Preston be by now, she wondered? She thought she had heard the sound of hooves in the courtyard a while ago, so she knew they had already departed. How long would it take for Alfie's sabotaged saddle straps to snap?

Stuck in the scullery, she became angry. Angry at Mr Preston, angry at the people who put her there, and angry at her own inability to do anything about it. The thought drove her

276

mad! Hot, bitter tears started welling up in her eyes.

No, she told herself as she wiped them away with her sleeve. *I mustn't think like that.*

She had to believe there was still time.

But what if there isn't?

What if it was too late already? What if Alfie lay in the dirt in a field somewhere, broken and dying? What would she do if she heard the news?

"Morning, Cook," the cheerful voice of Pete sounded in the kitchen, instantly snapping Stella out of her dark and fearful thoughts.

"Morning, love," Cook replied. "Feel free to help yourself to one of those apples on the table."

"I think I will, thank you. Being out in the fresh air makes you hungry."

"Being a strapping young lad is what makes you hungry," Cook laughed. "Tell me if you still want something after you've finished your apple, and I'll cut off a nice thick slice of fresh bread. I might even put some butter on it for you."

"Thanks, Cook."

Stella was standing in the open doorway to the scullery, and tried to get his attention. "Psst, Pete," she whispered.

Taking a big bite out of his apple, he turned round and seemed surprised to see her there. She beckoned him to come over.

"Morning, Stella," he nodded, a bit apprehensively. "What can I do for you?"

He was strangely business-like and distant she noticed. Not like his usual jovial self at all.

"I came to look for you in the stables earlier," she said hesitantly.

A painful grin appeared on his face. "Ah, is that why you were in the stables then?"

She frowned. "What? Are you telling me you saw me there?"

"No. But Tommy did."

Oh, heavens no!

"He told me he saw you leaving the stables together with Mr Preston. After you'd been up in the hay loft."

Her old friend seemed genuinely hurt.

"Pete," she begged. "That's not true. You have to believe me, please. In the name of the friendship we once had."

"All right. You've got time to convince me until I've finished this apple. Start talking." Somewhat defiantly, he took another bite from his apple and looked at her, waiting.

"I went over to the stables because I wanted to talk to you. I'd just had a chat with you father, and he made me see more sense about... you and I."

She blushed, but then she remembered they couldn't afford to lose any more time, so she pressed on.

"But when I got to the stables, you weren't there. I only saw Atlantis and another horse, ready for their ride. And then I saw Mr Preston coming, so–"

I can't tell him about that night when Mr Preston tried to– Not now at least.

"So I decided to hide in the hay loft. To avoid... being caught."

"Okay. Go on." Pete was beginning to nibble at the edges of his apple core.

"And that's when I saw– When I overheard– Oh, Pete, it's dreadful!"

Her panic made him stop eating. "What? What happened? What did you see?"

She grabbed him by his sleeve and whispered, "Pete, I saw him cut Alfie saddle straps."

"He did what?!"

"Shh, keep your voice down. He took out his knife and cut those straps so they would snap during their ride."

"But why?"

"Because he wants Alfie to have an accident. A fatal accident."

Pete's eyes grew wide with shock and disbelief.

"He wants Alfie dead, Pete. I heard him say so."

"That dirty rotten scoundrel!"

"So you believe me?"

"Course I do," he nodded. "Preston is perfectly capable of committing such a disgusting act. That man hates Alfie even more than Mrs Bosworth does."

"And Tommy's lie about me and Mr Preston up in the hay loft?" She blushed with shame, but she had to ask.

"The moment Tommy told me that crazy story, I knew there had to be something else to it."

She could have cried with joy and relief.

"We must save Alfie, Pete."

"Have you told anyone yet?"

"Who would believe me? Cook? Mrs Burch?" She grimaced. "Mrs Bosworth?"

"You're right." He thought for a heartbeat and then said, "I guess that means we'll have to save him ourselves."

"How?"

"We'll take one of the horses and go after them. I know the places where Mr Preston likes to ride."

"So you do care about him," she said with a warm smile on her face.

"What?" Pete looked confused.

"You still care about Alfie."

"Of course I do. He's my friend, isn't he?"

She could have hugged him then and there. But there wasn't any time for that now.

"Come to the stables with me," he said, taking her by the hand. "If we hurry, no one will notice until we're gone."

"Cook won't let me go though."

"I'll distract her, so you can slip outside. Wait for me at the stables."

He gave her a quick kiss and went into the main kitchen. Strolling over to the cooking range, he lifted up a few lids of the pots that stood simmering there.

"Hmm, this smells delicious, Cook. Mind if I have a little taste?"

"You cheeky rascal," Cook laughed. "Yes, I do mind." She waddled over to him, and gave him a good-natured slap on the wrist.

Behind her back, Pete saw Stella tiptoe towards the kitchen door. His distraction was working.

"I wouldn't have any dinner left," Cook chuckled. "Not if I let a young and greedy wolf like you taste my food while it's still on the fire. Let me make you some buttered toast instead."

Out of the corner of his eye, Pete could see Stella was outside and dashing for the stables.

"Don't bother, Cook," he smiled. "I'll save my appetite for whatever delicious delicacies you've got prepared for us later. Toodle-pip!" He doffed his cap to her, and left the kitchen.

Once he had caught up with Stella, the two of them ran over to the stables as if their lives depended on it.

Or rather, Alfie's life.

Chapter Thirty-Two

Everything seemed to be happening twice as fast when Stella and Pete came hurrying into the stables. But at the same time, the urgency of the moment created a remarkable clarity in Stella's head. It felt like she knew exactly what they needed to do to save Alfie. Step by step, it was all clear to her. It caused her to feel calmer than she ought to, she thought.

Pete grabbed a saddle, hung a bridle over his shoulder and went to one of the stable boxes.

"Nixie will help us, won't you, girl?" he spoke in that friendly voice he always used with the horses. "She's one of the fastest we have around here."

Swiftly, he placed the saddle on the horse's back and tightened the girth. Then he slipped the bridle over her head with what seemed like the greatest ease, and closed all the leather straps.

Nixie sensed Stella and Pete were in a nervous hurry, but she clearly trusted her handler and she remained calm throughout the lightning quick preparation.

Pete led the horse out of the box, hopped into the saddle and then held out his hand to Stella.

Frozen in place, she stared at his outstretched hand and at the horse that seemed awfully high all of a sudden. Her heart began to beat like a drum.

"Come on," he urged her. "Give me your hand and I'll pull you up behind me. Nixie can carry the two of us."

"I... I've never ridden a horse before."

"That's all right. I'll do the riding. You just hold on to me. Nixie is a good horse. Trust me, Stella."

His tone was urgent, but his eyes were friendly. And as she stared into them deeply, she knew she could trust him. She trusted him with her life.

So she gave him her hand, and he gripped it. With a grunt, and some effort from both of them, he pulled her up behind her.

"Don't let go," he told her after she had wrapped her arms around his waist.

I wouldn't dream of it, she thought, not daring to look how high above the ground they were sitting.

Pete pressed his heels into Nixie's sides and the horse walked towards the large stable doors.

"Where are you two going?" a flabbergasted Tommy asked when he saw them coming out of the stables.

"Urgent business, mate," Pete said. "Do me a favour and don't tell anyone until I get back, yeah?"

"You owe me for this, you randy devil," Tommy grinned.

Deciding not to waste any more time, Pete spurred their horse into a fast trot and made for the trees in the distance.

Meanwhile, on the other side of the forest, Alfie was sweating and panting while trying to keep up with Mr Preston. His mother's fiancé was driving them hard.

"Can't we let the horses walk for a while, Mr Preston?" he pleaded. "Atlantis loves to jump and gallop, but maybe they might want to have a bit of a rest as well?"

"Nonsense," Mr Preston called back, his own cheeks red from the heat and the exertion of their ride. "These horses are still as fresh as they were when we set out this morning. Are you sure it isn't you who wants some rest?"

"Perhaps. But we've been riding for so long, and quite strenuously too."

"Strenuously, eh? Good Lord, boy! You almost sound like those stuffy books you read. We need to grow you a proper backbone."

Alfie shot him a hateful look.

"If you say so, Mr Preston. Nevertheless," he insisted, "I feel my saddle is beginning to sit a little too loose. Perhaps we should stop, so I can dismount and adjust the girth."

Charles Preston halted their horses and glanced down at Alfie's saddle. "Loose, you say? Probably just your horse sweating. Nothing to concern yourself about."

"But Mr Preston–"

"Tell you what. See those hedges over there? Let's dash over there, jump over them for the fun of it, and then we can take a breather. If you promise not to tell your mother, I'll even let you have a sip from the small flask of brandy I've got in my pocket."

He winked at Alfie and dug his heels firmly into his horse's flanks. "Last one there is a pansy!"

Alfie sighed.

"Let's go, Atlantis. Once more unto the breach, dear friend, once more."

Elsewhere, Stella was beginning to lose hope. They had been racing across the countryside, but so far, they hadn't seen any sign or trace of Alfie or Mr Preston.

"It's useless, Pete. We'll never find them before it's too late. They've been out riding for so long."

"The countryside's a big place," he replied calmly.

He had halted briefly when they came out of another clearing, and now he was scanning the landscape in the faraway distance for the two riders they were pursuing.

"But we've been in every direction," she sighed, sounding more desperate than she wanted to. "And we've searched all of Mr Preston's favourite riding locations."

"Not all of them."

The determined look on his face and the resolute tone in his voice restored some of her own courage.

He turned round in the saddle to look at her over his shoulder and said, "There's one more place I want to try. It's where the brook runs through some fields, and it's got several hedges. Preston loves to jump over obstacles. Makes him feel manly."

"Good," she nodded. "Let's go there then."

Pete urged Nixie into a trot again.

Firmly clinging on to his waist, Stella asked, "Why do you think Mr Preston wants to kill Alfie?"

"Huh?" Pete called back.

"I said, why does he want Alfie dead? I know he hates him, but why would he want to kill him?"

"Money probably. That's usually what drives people like Preston. If Alfie's dead, his mother gets everything. And if Preston marries her, then what's hers becomes his."

Stella felt sick to the stomach. And it wasn't because of the bumpy horse ride.

"We have to find them, Pete! We simply must."

"We will," he shouted. "Hiyaah, Nixie. Faster, girl! Atlantis needs you."

Chapter Thirty-Three

"See if that tired old bag of bones of yours can beat that, you podgy bookworm!" Mr Preston taunted while he waved at Alfie from the other side of the brook he had just cleared.

Alfie exhaled angrily between gritted teeth.

"Did you hear that, Atlantis? He called you a tired old bag of bones. We'll show that saucy fellow, won't we, my trusted friend?"

He spurred his horse into a gallop and sent it racing towards the low hedge that stood on the near side of the brook. He knew Atlantis was big and strong enough to clear both the hedge and the brook. They just needed to develop sufficient speed to make the leap and get across safely.

Leaning forward, Alfie could hear the fast and deep breaths that were pumping through Atlantis' chest and nostrils. He could almost feel the physical power and the strength of his horse as its legs pounded the earth underneath them.

"Here we go," he shouted right before Atlantis thrust his hind legs against the ground, sending them flying through the air.

Then however, the events turned into a confusing blur for Alfie. He was surprised to feel himself falling off. He thought he caught a brief glimpse of Atlantis' legs and belly.

"That's not right," his mind registered in a surreal moment that seemed to last much longer than it actually did.

The next thing he knew, he crashed down onto the bank of the brook with a sickening thud, continued to roll, and splashed into the rushing water.

The world went black and he passed out briefly.

When Alfie opened up his eyes again, the first thing he noticed was a sharp pain in his left leg.

The second thing he noticed was Mr Preston sitting on his horse and staring down at him.

"Alfie, are you all right? That was quite a nasty tumble you took there."

"I can't move my leg," he groaned painfully. "And it hurts terribly. I think it might be broken."

"That's a shame," Mr Preston replied drily. "I had rather hoped you would break your bloody neck."

"Mr Preston, this is hardly the time for your jokes, I should think." Alfie whimpered as another flash of pain shot through his leg. "Please help me out of here."

But Mr Preston didn't move and stayed on his horse. "The water's cold then, is it?"

"Yes, very," Alfie answered angrily. Why didn't this man understand the seriousness of the situation? "I'm wet, I'm cold and my leg is hurting. Oh, and I'm lying in a brook filled to the brim with muddy water in case you hadn't noticed."

"Good. I guess that's an acceptable plan B."

"What on earth are you talking about? This isn't funny anymore, Mr Preston!"

"I know, my boy. Tragic, that's what it is. Deeply tragic. Lying in that cold, murky water with a broken leg like that? You'll catch your death before anyone gets to you."

Alfie wondered if perhaps the man had completely lost his mind. Or if he was merely being his usual cruel self.

Mr Preston shook his head. "No, I'm afraid the search and rescue party will never find you in time." He grinned sinisterly and continued, "Especially since I'll make sure to personally lead them far away from here for as long as I can."

Alfie gasped in utter shock and terror. "You want me to die out here?"

"My dear boy, of course I do. Why else do you think I sabotaged the straps of your saddle girth?"

"You did what?!"

"That's why you fell off just now. The straps snapped and whoops, you went flying. Not hard enough though unfortunately. Still, time will finish off the job."

"But why?"

"Come on, Alfie. I thought you were clever. Can't you figure it out? If you're dead and I marry your mother, all of your father's inheritance will be mine."

"You're even more evil than I thought, Mr Preston!"

"Thank you, that's very kind of you. I'm sure your mother will be very sad when she hears you're dead. Guess I'll have to comfort her."

"My mother will never believe you when you tell her it was an accident."

Mr Preston scoffed. "Your mother is ultimately just as weak as you are. Poor little Alfred. She merely wanted to break your spirit, you know. So she could control you. But that wasn't good enough for me. My plan is better. Obviously."

"It will never work! Someone will find me and then I'll tell everyone. And you–" Alfie tried to stand up, but his broken leg quickly caused him to change his mind. "Ow, my leg!"

"Hmm, yes. Good luck with that. Anyway, it's been lovely chatting with you but I'd better be off now."

He turned his horse around and manoeuvred it over to where Atlantis stood looking at his young master. With his crop whip, he lashed out viciously at Alfie's horse a few times, until the poor and frightened animal fled.

"Atlantis!" Alfie shrieked.

"Don't worry," Mr Preston laughed. "He'll find his way back to the estate eventually. You won't though. Because you'll be dead."

"You treacherous villain!"

"Cheerio, Alfred Bosworth. I think I'll ride back slowly – to give you more time to die."

Sneering and waving at Alfie, Mr Preston kicked his heels into the sides of his horse and trotted off.

"Come back, you miscreant! ," Alfie shouted. "Don't leave me here. Anybody, help!"

He yelled and cursed at Mr Preston until the man had disappeared from view.

"Miserable wretch."

When it was clear the lowlife wouldn't be coming back, he took stock of the predicament he was in. First, he needed to get out of this brook. Mr Preston had been right. He would catch his death in the cold, deep water. Hypothermia, they called it. He remembered that from one of his books.

He tried to climb the steep and muddy bank several times. But his broken leg hampered his every move, and the banks were very slippery because of the heavy rainfall they'd had all week long.

Finally, exhausted and wincing with pain, he gave up. He leaned with his back against the slippery bank, slid down deeper into the water, and cried.

Mr Preston had won. He was going to die.

Before he closed his eyes, and as the numbing cold crept further into his flesh, his thoughts were of Stella and Pete.

Chapter Thirty-Four

Just out of sight of the estate, Charles Preston stopped and dismounted. He tied his horse to a tree, and looked at the ground around him. Bending down, he dug both his hands into the mud. Then he smeared dirt all over his clothes, and even onto his face.

"I'm told some women pay good money for mud baths, old boy," he told his horse. "I don't see the attraction. But we need to make this look convincing, don't we?"

After he had ruffled up his hair until it looked like an exploded bird's nest, he took out his hunting knife. Holding his breath, he made a small cut in his own finger. Grimacing, he smeared some blood in his face.

"The things I do for love," he sniggered. "Or rather, money."

He put his knife away and walked back to his horse.

"There. What do you think, old boy? Does it look as if I fell off too? Now all I have to do is act like I've witnessed a terrible tragedy. After all, my dear fiancée's son has fallen to his death."

Laughing, he got on his horse again and made it trot for the last short stretch of their journey back to the estate.

"Charles!" Mrs Bosworth shouted frantically as soon as he came into view. She was standing in the courtyard, surrounded by a small group of stable hands and other staff members including the housekeeper Mrs Burch. One of the boys was holding Atlantis, who was naturally missing his saddle.

"Charles, what's happened? When Alfie's horse returned without you, we were so worried."

He trotted right up to them, and then let himself slide off his own horse, seemingly exhausted. When his feet reached the ground, his legs gave out and buckled, no longer able to support his weight.

Mrs Bosworth hurried over and dropped down by his side. "My poor Charles," she wailed, holding him in her arms while stroking his disheveled hairdo. "And where's my Alfred?"

"Josephine," he replied faintly. "It was horrible. Alfie fell."

"My baby! Where? What happened? Oh Charles, please tell me!"

"Water," he croaked. "My throat is so dry."

"Bring him a glass of water," Mrs Bosworth snapped.

Someone rushed off and brought back a glass and a jug of water. When he had taken a few slow and careful sips, Mr Preston sighed.

"We were riding, very calmly, enjoying the peaceful scenery, and then–"

He took another sip of water, and suddenly sucked in air as an invisible and non-existing injury caused him pain.

"You said my Alfred fell?"

Mr Preston nodded. "Atlantis," –he swallowed heavily– "He got spooked by a hare, or something. I think. All I remember is both our horses then panicked. Mine reared and threw me off. Ow, my ribs!"

He winced, and Mrs Bosworth took his hands.

"I'll be fine, my love," he said. "Alfie managed to stay in his saddle at first. You should have seen our boy, Josephine. He was so brave. But then..."

He paused, too overcome with emotion to continue.

"Go on. What happened then?"

"Atlantis bolted, and Alfie– Oh Josephine, I'm so sorry. I saw Alfie fall, and I fear– I fear he's dead!"

"No no no no no! That can't be! Not my baby boy. Not my darling Alfred! Where is he now? Did you leave him out there all by himself?"

"His broken body seemed lifeless, Josephine. There was nothing I could do for him."

"We need to find him!"

"Of course. I will personally lead a group of men to the place where it happened." He touched his painful head. "That is–"

He paused as a worried frown appeared on his brow.

"What is it, Charles?"

"If I can remember the precise location, that is. I took such a bad fall myself, my mind still seems a bit fuzzy. But not to worry, it will come back to me once we're on the trail, I'm sure."

"Mr Draper," she yelled at her head coachman. "Assemble the men. You will all set off to rescue my son immediately."

"Josephine, he's dead, my love. I've seen it with my own eyes. Just give me a few more moments and I shall be back on my feet."

"Don't believe a word that scoundrel is saying, Mother," the voice of Alfred Bosworth shouted from afar.

Every head turned.

There, approaching the yard while sitting astride Nixie's back, with Pete and Stella walking on either side of the horse to steady the injured rider, was Alfie – looking very determined, and very angry.

"Alfie," Mrs Bosworth cried, tears of relief and delight streaming down her face. Forgetting all about her fiancé, she ran over to her son, her skirts flying behind her.

The group of people around her followed, including Charles Preston, who seemed to have recovered miraculously.

Pete helped Alfie down from the horse, just when Mrs Bosworth reached them. Mother and son fell in each other's arms.

"Oh, my sweet darling Alfie," she said, raining kisses all over his face. "Charles thought you were dead."

"I would have been," Alfie replied, staring hard at Mr Preston. "If Pete and Stella hadn't found me."

"We found him lying in a brook, ma'am," Stella said. "With a broken leg."

"I'm so sorry, Alfie," Mrs Bosworth sobbed. "I never should have let you go riding with him. I knew it was too dangerous from the start."

"It's especially dangerous," Pete said, "when someone cuts the straps of your saddle girth."

Mrs Bosworth looked at him. "What are you saying? And what were you two doing out there in the first place?"

"Pete and Stella came to rescue me, Mother. After they found out Mr Preston wanted to murder me?"

"Murder?!"

"Now look here," Charles Preston bristled. "The boy has clearly suffered a nasty blow to the head and doesn't know what he's saying. I would never dream of harming him. You know that,

Josephine darling. I love him as if he were my own flesh and blood."

"You're a liar," Alfie growled darkly.

"Josephine, don't listen to him, I beg you. The boy was always against you and me. Against our love. And now he's trying to drive us apart with these outrageous lies. Aided and abetted by these two." He pointed an arrogant finger at Stella and Pete.

Mrs Bosworth looked from her fiancé to her son and the two servants, her eyes full of doubt.

Stella took a bold step forward.

"I can vouch for every word your son is saying, ma'am." She tried to steady her voice, which was trembling with anger and fear.

"With my own eyes, I saw Mr Preston cut those straps on Alfie's saddle. And with my own ears, I overheard him talking about his evil plan. He wanted your son to have a deadly accident."

"More lies," Mr Preston screamed. "Scandalous slander from a rejected, jealous maid."

Mrs Bosworth raised an eyebrow. "Rejected? Jealous?"

Mr Preston nodded and hung his head. "I wasn't going to tell you this, but a while ago, that little minx over there tried to seduce me. Needless to say, I turned her down. She got angry with me and vowed to have her revenge. I suppose this vicious lie is exactly that."

Everyone looked at Stella.

"You evil, lying serpent," she yelled at him. "It was you who tried to have your wicked way with me when I'd gone to the privy that night. It was you who told me I wouldn't be able to refuse you anymore once you were master of this house."

Suddenly, out of nowhere, Pete shot forward and planted a fist square in Mr Preston's face. The vile man shrieked with pain, and then covered his bleeding, broken nose with his hand.

"Enough!" Mrs Bosworth commanded. "I demand to know the truth."

"The truth, Mother," Alfie said calmly, "is that Charles Preston wanted me dead. He cut my saddle straps, hoping I would fall to my death. And when I merely broke my leg, he left me behind in that brook, knowing I would eventually die from shock and hypothermia."

Mrs Bosworth didn't say a word. Slowly, she took one step away from her fiancé, scrutinising him with those cold, blue-grey eyes of hers.

"And he told me all this as I lay there in the brook, Mother. Thinking I wouldn't live to tell the tale. He wants to control father's wealth himself."

All eyes were on Mrs Bosworth now.

Mr Preston reached out his hands to her, pleading, his face smiling and sweet. "My beautiful Josephine, these three are nothing but poor, misguided young fools who wish to ruin our happiness."

Mrs Bosworth held up her hand to cut him off.

"Charles," she spoke calmly. "You will pack your belongings and disappear from our lives. I never wish to see you again."

"But darling—"

"If you aren't gone from this estate in one hour, I shall have the police arrest you for the attempted murder of my son."

Realising his game was up, he looked darkly at everyone and then turned around, heading for the main house.

"See to it that he packs and leaves," Mrs Bosworth instructed one of the footmen.

Once her former fiancé had disappeared from view, all strength seemed to desert her. Reaching for her housekeeper's arm, she whispered, "Mrs Burch, I think I shall require a pot of strong tea, please."

"Certainly, ma'am."

With great care, Mrs Bosworth was escorted inside, leaving Alfie behind with Stella and Pete.

"I suppose I'd better go with her," Alfie said. "She will want to hear the full story."

"You do that, Alfie," Pete nodded.

"Will I find you two at the stables later?"

"Of course you will," Stella smiled.

Chapter Thirty-Five

When the commotion and excitement finally died down at the Bosworth estate, Stella took a deep breath and exhaled. She and Pete had needed to tell their side of the event over and over again, in every possible detail, for the gathered staff. People kept asking questions, and they wanted to hear the story several times. Initially, to understand it better – but then because they couldn't get enough of a tale so juicy and so scandalous. It would be the rumour of the decade they said. The story of the rich widow's fiancé trying to murder her son to get his greedy hands on the inheritance.

The evening sky was turning different shades of orange, red and violet by the time Stella and Pete managed to escape to the stables. Cook had slipped them a folded towel with bread and sausage, and biscuits. And just as they left, Mr Draper had pushed a jug of ale into Stella's hands, with a smile and a friendly wink.

The two of them feasted in private, giggling and talking. Pete had insisted on rubbing down and brushing the three horses all by himself.

"After a day like today, I owe them at least that much," he said.

But that was fine by Stella. She understood it was his way of winding down. And she liked to watch him care for the horses. He was so gentle with them. It helped to calm her own mind as well.

He was nearly done brushing the last of the three horses, when she leaned back lazily against a bale of hay and sighed.

"Thank you," she said.

"What for?"

"For believing me this morning when I told you about what Mr Preston was planning."

"Stella, the day we met I knew you were honest. The kind of girl I knew I could trust – always."

His words felt like a healing balm to her heart. They gave her the courage to bring up the other thing that was on her mind.

"And thank you for believing me when Mr Preston lied about..." She hesitated. "You know, about what happened that night when he–"

"Hey, I know his kind." Pete put away his brush, and came to sit next to her. "Preston is the rich and privileged sort. The master who thinks he can have his ways with every woman and girl in the household."

"Good thing our new master is a very different kind then, eh?"

"Yeah, Alfie is going to make a fine husband to a very lucky woman someday."

They both smiled, and then a happy silence fell between them.

"Pete? Why did you punch Mr Preston?"

He shrugged. "The man had it coming."

"Oh, absolutely. He deserved to get punched in that smug face of his. Don't get me wrong. It's just that you didn't strike me as the violent type."

"I'm not," he chuckled. "Not usually anyway. But I hate it when a man tries to take advantage of a woman."

"Ah, so you're a gallant knight then?"

She giggled. Even more so when she noticed him blushing slightly.

"Maybe," he said. "I would stand up for any girl or woman's honour, I guess."

"But would you go round punching nasty men in the face?"

They both laughed.

"Not all of them," he said.

"So why did you punch Mr Preston?"

"When I heard what he had tried to do to you, something inside me snapped. I got angry. Because you're special."

"I'm special?"

He looked her in the eyes, and said, "To me you are."

Under different circumstances, they might have laughed and giggled at this exchange of theirs. But now the mood was different. Something hung in the air between them. It was simultaneously a peaceful silence because everything that needed to be said had been said – and an exhilarating tension, because they both sensed something needed to happen.

Slowly, and while taking delight in the moment, their faces inched closer together. She was feeling fuzzy and tingly in her head. Whether that was due to the events earlier that day, the ale they had drunk, or simply his mesmerisingly close presence, she didn't know.

And she didn't care either. All she knew was that she liked being near to him.

Their lips were tantalisingly close to each other, within touching distance, ready for that liberating kiss.

"Good heavens," Alfie sighed heavily as he entered the stables. "I thought Mother would never stop asking me questions."

Blushing and clearing their throats, Stella and Pete quickly pulled away from each other.

Not seeming to have noticed anything, Alfie continued his babbling. "I swear she and I have talked more to each other these past few hours than in the last five years."

"But you're all good though, right?" Stella asked, trying to appear casual as she brushed off some hay from her dress. "I mean, your mother isn't angry with you or anything, is she?"

Out of the corner of her eye, she saw Pete shifting on the bale of hay they were sitting on. She didn't want him to get up, so she took his hand, folded her hands around his, and rested them in her lap.

"No, not all," Alfie replied. "We have had a very good conversation. I spoke my mind, and she apologised for her behaviour."

"She apologised?" Pete asked incredulously. "That must have been a first."

Stella squeezed his hand, and discreetly shook her head at him. Now wasn't the time for jokes or sarcasm.

But Alfie took it well. He smiled and said, "I know. I could hardly believe my own ears when she did. It's all going to be different from now on."

"That's nice to hear," Stella answered.

"She and I are going to make my work schedule lighter again. And she wants to bring in tutors and mentors who will prepare me for the task of managing our family estate and assets."

"Wow," Pete said. "It really does sound like she's had a complete change of heart."

Alfie nodded vigorously. "Oh, and Stella? You have been reinstated as a regular house maid. I insisted."

"That's wonderful, Alfie! Thank you."

Hopping to her feet, she rushed over to him with her arms open, and placed a big sisterly kiss on his cheek. He blushed, which made Pete laugh.

Still glowing from her kiss, Alfie continued, "I am so happy everything will once again be like before."

"So are we, Alfie," Stella said, as she went back over to Pete, sat down next to him and put his hand in her lap again.

"We will still need to be somewhat discreet about our friendship naturally," Alfie said slightly awkwardly. "Mother won't be so overbearing and domineering anymore. But apparently, the master isn't supposed to be seen being friends with the staff." He rolled his eyes. "Stupid conventions."

"That's okay, Alfie," Pete grinned. "The three of us will always be friends, no matter what the world thinks."

Stella looked at him, and beamed. She was over the moon to hear those words coming from him.

Again, silence fell over them. Alfie smiled at his two friends, and they smiled back.

Then, Alfie's gaze settled on Stella's hands holding Pete's hand in her lap. And the penny dropped.

"Anyway," he said, trying to sound every inch of the confident master of the house. "It's been a long day, and I'm sure we're all very tired. So I shall leave you to it."

He cleared his throat, and looked about him, not entirely sure about the correct way to make a graceful exit.

"Thank you for coming round, Alfie," Stella smiled. "We're looking forward to your next visit."

"Of course. Oh, and thank you both, once again, for saving me today."

"It's what friends do," Pete said. "Good night, Alfie."

"Good night." He turned round and headed for the door, waving happily. "See you soon."

Once he was gone, Pete turned to Stella with a broad grin on his face. "Now, where were we?"

"I believe you were about to kiss me, Pete Draper."

"Oh yeah, that's right."

He took her in his arms, and finally, their lips met in the warmest and most loving embrace she had ever known.

Chapter Thirty-Six

As the most senior maid of the house, Stella inspected the younger girls, who were all lined up neatly in a row in the grand reception room, keeping their eyes forward and waiting for their final instructions before the big event.

Carefully and diligently, she looked at each and every one of them. She checked if their uniforms were tidy, with their caps sitting nice and straight on their heads, and whether they held themselves with the right combination of modest confidence and friendly dignity.

Finishing her inspection, she stood in front of them and smiled. "You all look perfect. And I want you to know I'm proud of you."

She thought she saw the girls grow a bit taller with joy and relief. Which in turn made her happy. Ever since Stella had become the eldest of the housemaids, Mrs Burch had given her more responsibility over the other maids. Stella had vowed to do things differently, with more kindness.

And her approach had evidently borne fruit.

The housekeeper entered the room as well, strictly business-like as usual. "Are you ready, Miss Reed?"

"We are all ready, Mrs Burch. And I can assure you the girls will perform their duties admirably."

"I am certain that they will, Miss Reed. You taught them well."

"Thank you, Mrs Burch."

"Now, ladies, if I may have your attention? I trust it has been impressed upon you just how important this occasion is in the life of the Bosworth family? It's Master Alfred's twenty-first birthday: the day he fully and legally comes into his father's inheritance, thereby becoming our master. You must each do your part in making this celebration a moment to remember."

"We shall not let the master and Mrs Bosworth down, Mrs Burch," Stella said. "Isn't that right, girls?"

"Aye, miss," the maids replied earnestly.

When Alfie and his mother came in, he smiled and nodded discreetly at Stella. And even

Mrs Bosworth seemed pleased to see the staff ready and waiting.

Shortly afterwards, the first guests arrived. The rest of the afternoon, Stella was busy serving drinks while keeping a watchful eye on *her* girls, who did indeed perform splendidly and without fault.

Hours later, after the last guest had left, she was exhausted. The staff had just started to clear up the room, when Mrs Burch called her over.

"Mr Bosworth would like to see you in his study at your earliest convenience, dear."

"But we haven't finished cleaning up yet."

"I'm sure the other maids can handle that by themselves. Why don't you go and see him now?"

Stella didn't like letting the others do all the dirty work, but then again, the master took priority.

She wiped her hands on a towel, checked her uniform in one of the mirrors and proceeded to Alfie's study.

"Stella," he greeted her cordially when she entered. He stood up from behind his large wooden desk.

"Alfie," she smiled after she had closed the door. "Pete?" She was surprised to see her fiancé sitting in one of the chairs. Wearing his Sunday best, he looked somewhat uncomfortable and out of place in the plush surroundings.

Alfie gestured at a chair next to Pete. "Please, sit down, Stella. Oh, and thank you for making my birthday party such a tremendous success."

"It wasn't just me," she replied modestly. "It was a team effort. The girls did well."

"That's because they learned from the best. Namely, you."

"Thank you." She blushed. Hearing words of praise still felt fairly new to her. Even though she knew she had earned them.

"I have invited you both here this evening, because I wanted to discuss some matters with you."

"You sound serious, Alfie," Pete said.

"One might say they're serious matters, my friend." He cleared his throat. "I have been told the two of you intend to be married?"

Stella smiled. "Yes, Pete has proposed to me!"

"Congratulations," Alfie beamed. "But may I ask, what will you do once you're married? Will you be staying on as our senior maid?"

"Unfortunately, no. I have decided to leave." She lowered her eyes. It was the most sensible decision, but that didn't make it any easier. "Married life is impossible to combine with my full-time position as a maid living in the house."

"I understand," Alfie said. "However, I shall be sad to see you go. I won't just be losing the best maid this family has ever had. I will also be losing a friend."

"We will always be friends, Alfie," Pete said. "You know that."

"And what about you, Pete? You aren't leaving too, are you?"

"I'm afraid so. I want to be more than just a stable boy. I'll have to," he chuckled, "if I want to support a family."

Stella assumed this double blow was hard for Alfie, but he kept up a brave face.

"Any idea yet what you want to do instead?"

"Not really," Pete said. "Something with horses, naturally. Maybe I'll start my own coach company, and breed a few horses on the side for the extra money."

"Will you be staying in London?"

Pete shrugged. "The city is an expensive place to live and work. We thought we might move to the country. More space to raise horses, and Stella could find work as a daily maid, working a few hours a day for a wealthy farmer perhaps."

Alfie pursed his lips. "Sounds like you might struggle a bit in the beginning. I mean, it won't be easy to start all over again in a place where you are strangers."

"Probably," she said. "But we prefer living in the countryside over the city." She smiled and added, "All those lovely summers at the estate did that to us."

Alfie was visibly disappointed. A deep frown appeared on his face, and Stella could tell that smart thinking brain of his was working hard.

As he sat there at his desk, staring out of the window, he completely looked the part of the wise and capable wealthy master of the house. And she felt proud of him. He had come such a long way.

"I have another proposition for you," he said eventually. "For both of you."

"Let's hear it," Pete nodded.

"I understand why you prefer the countryside over the city. And I admire that you want to get ahead in life. On the other hand, I'd hate to lose two of my most valued and trusted members of staff."

"It was a difficult decision for us as well, Alfie," Stella said.

"Which is why I want you two to run the Buckinghamshire estate."

Stella blinked in disbelief. Surely, he was joking?

"Come again?" Pete echoed her confusion.

"I want you, Pete, to take charge of the horses, the stables, the breeding – the whole lot. If it's anything to do with horses, you'll run the show."

While Pete was left dumbstruck, Alfie turned to Stella.

"And I want you, Stella, to be the permanent housekeeper of the manor. There's always a small number of staff present to maintain the house, and in the summer, well, you know what the summers are like."

"Alfie, we're honoured," Pete stammered. "But..."

He didn't know how to finish his sentence. So Stella finished it for him. "But it's too much."

"Too much?"

"Don't you think Pete and I are a bit too young and inexperienced for such a great responsibility?"

Alfie laughed. "You're asking me? The 21-year-old who just took legal possession of a vast family fortune with business dealings, properties and land all over Britain?"

"But that's different," Stella argued.

"Yeah, Alfie. You've got staff and lawyers and clerks and Lord knows who else to help you run it all."

Alfie folded his hands in front of him and looked at them. "And so will you. I have come to realise that leading other people often means first asking them for their opinion and their advice, and then deciding what you think is best."

"That may be, but–"

"And I know you are both smart enough, kind enough and brave enough to do what you feel is right."

"But what if we let you down?"

"You won't."

"You seem very certain about that."

"You have never let me down before. And I know that you never will."

"We might if we make a mistake."

Alfie shrugged. "To err is human. And if it's anything truly important or costly, then you simply consult with me first."

Stella could see he was deadly serious about this idea of his. "When did you become so determined and self-assured?" she quipped.

"I owe much to the support of some very good friends," Alfie replied. "So what do you say to my proposal?"

"It's very tempting," Pete said.

"Is there any reason why you would want to refuse?"

Stella and Pete looked at each other. Neither of them could think of any valid excuse.

"It... It sounds like a dream," she hesitated.

"Not a dream," Alfie said. "Consider it my wedding gift to you. A symbol of our friendship. A friendship that once saved my life."

On the day our love was sealed, Stella thought as she stared at her future husband by her side.

"We accept," she and Pete both said at the same time, causing them to laugh at their synchronicity.

"Splendid!" Alfie exclaimed, elatedly throwing his arms up in the air. "I will have my solicitors draw up the paperwork in the morning."

He stood up and came round to their side of the table to shake their hands.

"On one condition of course," he spoke solemnly.

"Name it," Pete said.

"That you have your wedding at the summer estate. And that I'm invited as well."

"I think we can arrange that," Stella teased.

Laughing, the three of them took hold of each other's hands and stood in a small circle, revelling in the joy of their friendship.

Nothing would ever destroy that which bound their hearts together.

Epilogue

Under a clear blue sky, and with the afternoon sunshine warming their faces, Stella looked at Pete. Her husband smiled at her, took her hand and squeezed it gently. They were happy, and they didn't need any words to express the love they felt for each other.

Behind them stood a long row of servants who, just like them, were waiting for the Bosworth family to arrive. Alfie would be spending the summer at his large countryside estate again, in the company of his wife and their two young children.

"Mummy," little Emma Draper asked. "How much longer do we have to wait?"

"The Bosworths should be here any moment now, my darling. You have both been very patient. I'm proud of you."

"In our last letter I promised Reginald I'd take him fishing in the brook," young John Draper said. "If they get here in time, can he and I go today, Mother?"

"I'm sure that'll be fine, angel."

"But remember, children," Pete said. "Mr and Mrs Bosworth are important guests, so—"

"Always be polite," the children finished off their father's sentence in unison.

"And address them as sir, Mr Bosworth, ma'am and Mrs Bosworth," John added after they had stopped giggling.

Just then, they could hear a carriage coming up the long stately drive to the estate.

"I bet that's grandpapa driving the coach," Emma whispered.

The expensive carriage pulled up to the entrance of the main house and came to a full stop as a slight cloud of dust settled behind it.

In the driver's seat at the front sat old Mr Draper, head coachman of the Bosworth family. Having secured the carriage and his reins, Pete's father smiled at his son and his daughter-in-law, not bothering to hide his pride at their success and respectable position.

Delighted to see her grandfather, little Emma couldn't help herself and gave him an excited wave. He wiggled his moustache at her by twitching his nose, which made her giggle.

Remembering her station, she quickly covered her mouth with her hand to muffle her giggling.

Stella didn't say anything and let it slip. She knew it was impossible to resist the cheeky charms of the Draper men.

Charlotte and Reginald Bosworth were the first to alight from the carriage. They knew they had to wait for their parents to come out as well before they could greet their friends. But the entranced expression on their faces already spoke of all the fun and adventures they were planning in their minds.

When Alfie got out, he closed his eyes and took a deep breath. "Aaah," he sighed as he exhaled and opened his eyes again. "Will you smell that fresh air, Amelia! Heavens above, it's good to be back. I can't wait to go out and paint in the open air."

"You're in luck, sir," Pete said. "The gorgeous weather is looking to hold out for a while longer. How is London?"

"Busier and smellier than ever, Pete. Say, I don't suppose you'd fancy trading places with me, would you?"

Pete laughed. "No, I think I prefer my life as a country bumpkin."

"You're hardly a country bumpkin," Alfie chortled. "A shrewd businessman and an equine genius is what you are. Have you seen our latest sales records? Those award-winning horses of yours are worth a small fortune."

"It's amazing what the right care and a little love will do," Pete smiled.

"Speaking of which, how is Atlantis?"

"Enjoying his well-deserved retirement out in the fields. Want to go and see him?"

"Of course! I hope the old boy will still recognise me."

"Oh, I'm sure he'll come running straight to you when he sees you. He's far too clever and loyal to ever forget the years of service and friendship you shared."

Listening in on their conversation, Alfie's daughter Charlotte came tugging at her father's sleeve. "And can we visit the baby horses, Papa?" she begged.

"Foals they're called, my little darling. Yes, you can. But first, let's go inside so we can change and have a light meal."

Leaning in closer towards Stella and Pete, he quietly added, "And so we can drop this 'sir' and 'Mr Bosworth' nonsense. I will never get used to you two calling me that."

They laughed, and Alfie threw an arm around Pete's shoulder as the men went up the broad stone steps that led to the main house, with all four children in tow.

Smiling, Stella and Amelia Bosworth stood watching their husbands who were chatting and joking with each other.

Dreamily gazing at her Alfred, Amelia said, "He really is a completely different person when we come out here, you know?"

"I've noticed," Stella replied. "And how are you, Mrs Bosworth?"

"Oh please, Stella. Call me Amelia. I'm only Mrs Bosworth in London."

They giggled and linked their arms together, as they too went up the stairs to the main house. Stella glanced over at her staff and smiled. She knew she could trust them to do a good job at unloading and unpacking the last pieces of luggage without her supervision.

"You will find the house perfectly in order," she informed her friend and mistress.

"I have no doubt about that whatsoever. You are an even better housekeeper than Mrs Burch back in London."

"You're too kind."

"No, it's true. I can see it in the staff as well. They double their efforts whenever the household moves here."

"But that's only because they enjoy the fresh air and being in the beautiful countryside."

Amelia stopped and looked at her. "No, it's because of you, Stella. They all love you. And they respect you."

Stella blushed. "Well, I guess it's like Pete said. The right care and a little love go a long way."

Glancing at the estate, Amelia said, "Alfie and I are very fortunate to have you and Pete to look after this paradise of ours."

"No, Pete and I are the fortunate ones. Alfie was so terribly generous to put us in charge of the summer estate."

"He told me you didn't want to accept his offer at first," Amelia chuckled.

"Of course not! It was such a tremendous responsibility. But he had complete faith in us right from the start."

"That's what friends do, Stella."

They stood and smiled at each other, both realising how blessed their lives were.

"But come," Amelia said. "Let's go inside now. Or those darling husbands of ours might decide to visit the horses in their finest attire."

"While our darling children climb the curtains and swing from the chandeliers in the parlour."

Giggling like schoolgirls, they linked arms again and went to join their happy little families.

The End

Continue reading...

If you enjoyed this book, you will love Hope Dawson's other romance stories as well.

Visit www.hopedawson.com for updates and to *claim your free digital book*.

Other titles by Hope:

The Forgotten Daughter
The Carter's Orphan
The Millworker's Girl
The Ratcatcher's Daughter
The Foundling With The Flowers
The Pit Brow Sisters
The Dockside Orphans
The Christmas Foundling
The Market Girl's Secret
The Blind Sibling

Printed in Great Britain
by Amazon